A Walk In The Parkin

Baker's Rise Mysteries

Book Seven

R. A. Hutchins

Copyright © 2022 Rachel Anne Hutchins

All rights reserved.

The characters, locations and events portrayed in this story are wholly the product of the author's imagination. Any similarity to any persons, whether living or dead, is purely coincidental.

Cover Design by Molly Burton at cozycoverdesigns.com

ISBN: 9798352312612

For the Culture Vultures, the History Buffs,
Wilderness Wanderers and Tireless Trekkers…

"Adventure Awaits!"

Message from the Author

Little did I know when I started writing this series of mysteries set in Baker's Rise, that a certain feisty little parrot with no filter would fly into readers' affections and find a spot to roost in their hearts, just as he has in my own!

I can't express how grateful I am to you, our Reader, not least for the fact that you have joined us on Flora and Reggie's adventures this far. I can't wait to see what they get up to next – though I think it's safe to say there will be murder involved!

Thank you so much for your kind reviews and generous support.

As a certain little bird would say – and I wholeheartedly agree – you're a corker!

Warmest Wishes

CONTENTS

If you follow this list in order, you will have made a perfect **Traditional Yorkshire Parkin cake** *to enjoy whilst you read!*

1)	List of ingredients:	1
2)	110g self-raising flour	8
3)	110g soft butter	15
4)	110g soft dark brown sugar	23
5)	225g medium oatmeal	31
6)	200g golden syrup	42
7)	55g black treacle	50
8)	2 tsp ground ginger	57
9)	1 tsp ground mixed spice	64
10)	2 medium eggs, beaten	71
11)	1 tbsp milk	78
12)	Pinch of salt	86
13)	**What you need to do:**	**94**
14)	Preheat the oven to 140C/120C fan/ Gas Mark 1.	101
15)	Grease and line a 20cm x 20cm square cake tin.	110
16)	Melt the butter, sugar, treacle and golden syrup in a pan over a gentle heat without allowing it to bubble.	117
17)	When they have melted together remove from the heat and allow to cool slightly.	126
18)	Sift in the dry ingredients into a mixing bowl and make a well in the centre.	136
19)	Gradually add the melted butter mixture to the bowl and fold together.	146

20) Pour in the beaten eggs and milk and combine together.	153
21) Pour the contents of the bowl into your baking tin.	160
22) Bake for 1.5 hours, however don't become too engrossed in your book as parkin can easily become dry and over baked!	166
23) Remove from the oven and leave in the tin for 20 minutes.	170
24) Tip onto a cake rack and leave to cool completely.	177
25) Wrap the parkin in greaseproof paper and store in a cake tin.	184
26) Keep it in the tin for between 1 and 7 days before you cut it to allow cake to develop.	190
27) Enjoy with a cup of tea and a great read!	194
Excerpt from "Fresh as a Daisy" – Lillymouth Mysteries Book One	201
Baker's Rise Mysteries Book Eight	209
Baker's Rise Mysteries Book Nine	211
New Series! The Lillymouth Mysteries	213
About The Author	215
Other books by this Author	217
Historical romance under the pen name Anne Hutchins	219

ONE

Flora felt the beads of sweat trickling down her forehead and behind her sunglasses, as her fingers tapped a staccato beat on the steering wheel. Had she known there would be a heatwave in northeast England this particular week, then she would of course have had the air conditioning in her old Audi fixed. As it was, even with all the windows down the inside of the car still felt hotter than the Sahara. Almost as hot as her anger.

"Well, now that we've stopped, why don't we all take a moment to cool down," Jean said, diplomatically, and Flora knew she was talking about more than the temperature.

"I just can't believe you brought them," Flora said,

directing her comment to Betty behind her, who at least had the grace to look sheepish.

The journey had started out well, less than an hour ago, when Flora had picked her three friends up at Betty's house, said goodbye to Harry, and they had set off on the relatively short journey to Yorkshire, and on what was meant to have been Flora's honeymoon. She was not married, though – not yet anyway – and her fiancé had already left straight after the joint wedding of their friends, to take some time to heal and to grieve in the highlands of Scotland.

All of that had been planned. What hadn't been planned was that twenty minutes into the journey, Flora would hear the rather familiar squawk of a little parrot she thought had been left safely with Harry for the week.

"My Flora! Get out of it!"

At first, she had just thought he was a familiar echo in her head, since barely a day had passed in the last year without the distinctive chatter of her constant companion. When the tone became more irate, however, and Betty had started a fake coughing from the back seat where she sat next to Jean, Flora had shared a questioning look with Tanya in the front.

"Ah, Betty, is there something you would like to share?" Tanya had asked, twisting to look at the women in the back, and then down to the source of the sound. In the footwell beside Betty's feet was a box covered in a tea towel. Funnily enough, it was almost an identical match to the one by Jean's feet. Glancing at her friend, Flora caught Tanya's cocked eyebrow and questioning gaze.

"No lass, just got a frog in my throat," Betty had said, eying Jean beside her with a slight shake of the head.

Flora had kept driving, until a distinct yap came from the box beside Jean's feet, proving once and for all that she wasn't imagining it, and that those weren't picnic baskets as Betty had assured her when they packed the car. Of course, the older woman had had her husband put the containers in so quickly, covering them over like a magician with a rabbit in his hat, and Flora had not initially had any inkling as to their true contents.

"Tina! Tina the terror!" the responding shriek came from beside Betty's ankles, and Flora had felt her annoyance grow as now the truth couldn't be denied.

"Goodness Betty, they must be boiling in there!" Flora had said, taking the next slip road and pulling into the car park of the main services outside Newcastle upon Tyne.

"Don't be silly," Betty had scolded, obviously seeing no point in hiding the truth any longer, "the carry cases have air vents, I sprayed the animals liberally with water before we zipped them up and I even soaked the towels in water and put them in the freezer before lying them on top. I'd put my money on it that those two little lovelies are the coolest of any of us in this fire box."

"Well, let's get out and have a breather," Jean said calmly, mopping her brow with a pretty embroidered handkerchief. There was little breeze, the motorway being too far from the northeast coastline to benefit from even any slight relief from the heat.

Flora peeled her sticky legs from the seat and ran her sweaty palms over her sundress. The other three women were already out of the car, and if their appearance were any indication of her own, then Flora knew she must look a sight. When she had left her little coach house, her hair had been freshly blow dried and Flora had even applied a tinted moisturiser to her face. Now, she could feel the strands plastered to her wet forehead and a decidedly greasy texture coating her cheeks. Accepting Betty's peace offering of one of the cold tea towels that had been hiding the animal carriers, Flora used it to wipe her face, feeling immediately better from its cooling effect.

A flap of wings and a blur of green, and a familiar weight landed on Flora's shoulder, "Don't be going anywhere," she muttered to the bird, who nuzzled her neck contentedly, "we aren't in Baker's Rise anymore."

"Adventure awaits!" Reggie shrieked, repeating the phrase Flora had taught him that weekend.

"I had meant for you and Harry," she replied, as if her little friend could understand, "a nice cosy adventure, in his and Betty's cottage and in the bookshop, not on tour with us ladies!"

"Cosy adventure! Tour!" Reggie parroted back happily, stretching his wings before settling back into the crook of her neck.

Flora stroked his head feathers gently, reluctantly acknowledging that Betty had been right, the little bird did feel refreshingly cool.

"I just don't understand why you've insisted on bringing them," Flora asked, when all four were seated on a bench, flasks of hot tea and cheese scones out for elevenses.

Betty readjusted little Tina, who was sitting on her lap

catching the crumbs which the woman was deliberately letting fall, "Well, I just thought about my Harry having to take her for walks," Betty said, giving Flora a side-eyed look to see if she was falling for it, "since he had the pneumonia, he's not as strong as he was, you know."

"Hmm," Flora squinted her eyes behind her sunglasses and shook her head slightly, "well, you know the man better than us, but he seemed fully recovered to me, Betty. Are you sure you didn't just think you'd miss Tina?"

"Oh alright then, yes, and you can't tell me that you wouldn't miss this little chap here," Betty smiled indulgently as she fed Reggie a huge crumb from her scone, where he sat on Tanya's shoulder next to her.

"Well, I would of course, but I'm not even sure the hotel accepts pets. When I phoned to change the booking from the honeymoon suite, the lady said they were just undergoing some sort of transition. New management, I think she mentioned," Flora sighed audibly, causing Jean to interject.

"Well, we're too far along to take them home," the older woman said, "we might as well bring them on holiday. More the merrier, hey?"

"I suppose so," Flora conceded.

"Then that's settled," Tanya smiled, standing and brushing crumbs briskly from her tiny shorts and causing both dog and bird to descend to the concrete to hoover them up, "let's get going before the day gets any hotter. This is my first holiday since I came to England and I'm sure I don't want to waste it in a service station car park!"

Flora tutted and stood slowly, though inside she felt her excitement for the trip return. Sea air, plenty of cups of tea accompanied by lots of cakes, and time to be a tourist for a few days.

It was just two extra in their little group, what could possibly go wrong?

TWO

The drive through the North Yorkshire moors was a rather smoky one, as off in the distance the women could see the outlines of firefighters trying to quell the small wildfires that had broken out amongst the gorse and heather in the unusually dry heat. The purples and whites of those same plants that now lined the single-lane road on which they drove were beautiful though, and Flora slowed as they came to the top of the hill that she knew led down into the town of Lillymouth.

The moors became fields on the left, and, driving on, the women passed a quaint train station on the right, at which Flora remembered the directions from the hotel receptionist were to turn right, towards the harbour and the north sea beyond. It almost pained Flora to leave the road before she reached what looked like a row of old fisherman's cottages, and the stone bridge over the fast flowing Lillywater river. Beyond that, Flora remembered from her research online, lay the town itself where the wife of the Baker's Rise vicar had told them her own friend was the parish incumbent – Daisy Bloom – and Sally had said they should ask for her at the vicarage during their stay.

Anyway, Flora thought as she made the sharp right turn, avoiding a random pheasant that was out for a daily jaunt, *there will be plenty of time to explore the town and to make new acquaintances tomorrow.* For today, she needed to navigate this tiny lane, past the Crow's Nest Inn as she had been directed, and to the hotel which stood on the cliff top overlooking the small harbour and the coastline. In olden times, so Flora had read, the town was a hubbub of fishing activity, and some smuggling too, though now only a few tourist cruisers and local boats were moored in the small harbour, protected by the twin piers which pointed out to sea.

"Isn't it beautiful!" Tanya exclaimed, stroking Reggie who had jumped from her lap to the woman's shoulder to look out of the window, detecting from her expression that there was something new to see.

"Adventure awaits!" the little bird squawked, bobbing

up and down happily.

"It really is," Jean agreed, "I've been to Yorkshire before, to Whitby and Scarborough, and inland to York of course, but I've never been to this particular spot."

"Aye, looks grand, let's see what the afternoon teas are like," Betty agreed as Flora pulled into a small, gravelled car park, and despite the fact it wasn't even lunchtime yet.

A relatively small manor house in Georgian design stood in front of them, not so unlike Flora's own building at The Rise. A large set of wooden doors stood open, behind an open brick porch that was held up by four columns.

"Very grand," Tanya agreed, as they all bundled out of the car, happy for the small sea breeze which they could now feel wafting over.

As Flora opened the boot for them to retrieve their luggage – all the while encouraging Reggie not to fly off ahead, lest he get himself into trouble before they'd even checked in and got permission for their surprise companions – she saw a petite, blonde haired woman emerge suddenly from a door at the side of the building. Untying her apron, ripping it over her head and flinging it behind her, she marched in their direction.

"Good afternoon," Flora smiled with not a small amount of uncertainty.

"Is it?" The woman asked sadly, her eyes full of unshed tears. Without pausing to hear an answer she stormed past, her advanced years belying the speed at which the woman could walk.

"Well, the locals are clearly as friendly as those in Baker's Rise," Tanya joked as they made their way towards the grand entrance.

"You're a corker!" Reggie agreed with her happily, keen to share the joke and coming to land on her friend's shoulder as Flora stepped forward to check the group in.

"Well, it could be worse," Jean said softly, though even she was eying the super king-sized bed with a completely sceptical expression.

"Worse than the four of us in the honeymoon suite and the animals relegated to the laundry room downstairs each evening and overnight?" Betty asked, picking up a handful of rose petals from the bed and throwing them like confetti over Jean's head.

"Well, at least the young woman on reception said they can convert the sofa in the little lounge area to a single, and add a camp bed, so that only leaves two of us sleeping in this one," Flora replied, though she herself didn't relish the prospect of the four women sharing the – admittedly large – space, especially not in this heat.

"Well, they have left prosecco and treats," Tanya said happily, sinking down onto one of the twin armchairs, "I've stayed in worse, much worse."

"Aye well, we should make the best of it," Betty said, eying the complimentary plate of Yorkshire parkins hungrily, "no point letting it go to waste. Let's get that tiny kettle on, and our shoes off."

"Yes, then when we're feeling refreshed we can go exploring," Jean said happily, stroking Tina who was looking at the tray of baked goods hopefully.

"They didn't seem too keen on us having the animals up here during the day, or in any of the reception rooms downstairs," Flora said, remembering the fierce scowl of the young woman on reception, who had begun sneezing the moment Tina was in her vicinity.

"Aye well, we'll be out most of the time anyway," Betty picked Tina up and cuddled her to her ample bosom, "it's bad enough they're to be shut away at night. As if these two would disturb the other guests!"

Flora looked at Reggie, sitting in the large bay window overlooking the harbour, scoffing green grapes from a Tupperware box that Betty had produced from her suitcase. When the older woman had also removed a small metal rod, which unfolded several times and popped together to form a perch, as if she was Mary Poppins with her carpet bag, Flora's eyes had been out on stalks.

"Well, you've come prepared Betty," Flora had said, somewhat incredulous.

"Aye well, I stowed them away, I didn't intend to deprive the little loves," Betty said, clearly a tad put out and removing pouches of dog food, dry kibble and a large box of seed from her luggage.

"You've done a great job, thank you," Flora said, calling a truce and putting her arm around her friend's shoulders, "though I think that grumpy woman at the front desk may have had a point about the noise. Reggie's not exactly known for his quiet moments!"

The women chuckled and enjoyed the stress-free

holiday feeling, whilst Flora sent a silent prayer heavenward that it would last.

THREE

"So that's the four of you booked onto the traditional parkin bakin' class in the new cake budio tomorrow at ben," the same young woman from earlier, whose badge identified her as Hailey, spoke whilst still typing and looking at the large computer screen on the front desk. Her words were punctuated with sneezes, though her fingers paused only briefly when she scowled at little Tina.

"Could you take the animals outside… pleab," the request was muffled by the congestion in her nose, and she made a show of taking a tissue from the box on the welcome desk where she sat.

"Well, I…" Betty began.

"Of course," Flora acquiesced quickly, handing Reggie's carrier to Tanya. Squawks of "Get out of it!" and "Where to now?" permeated the thin canvas cover, and Flora felt her cheeks heating. Tanya also took hold of the little terrier's lead and strode off towards the main doors, her newly-red, curled locks bouncing, in stark contrast to her skimpy white bustier. Apparently, Tanya hadn't got the Lillymouth memo, as she was surely dressed for Lanzarote!

"Now Betty, are you sure you and I want to be taking baking lessons – after all, we're normally the ones doing the teaching. How will you manage to bite your tongu… ah, to not get bored?" Jean asked pointedly.

"Well, we're in Yorkshire, and I want to see how they make their local cakes," Betty exclaimed, raising her hands in a gesture of exasperation as if this should be obvious, and perhaps deliberately missing the essence of the question.

"Okay, so that's definitely four of you?" Hailey asked, apparently equally exasperated with the group, and flicking bits of dried paint from her short-sleeved blouse and exposed forearms as if she had long since become bored with the conversation.

"Yes, thank you, please add it to my bill," Flora spoke on a sigh, worrying that her little group had not given the best impression in the single hour they'd been at the hotel. She would've been happy to put her feet up for a bit longer before they started exploring the town, but one quick cuppa and the others were chomping at the bit to get going.

"Very well. Ingrid likes to start at ten sharp. All aprons and ingredients will be provided." And with that they were effectively dismissed.

Flora wondered briefly if Ingrid had been the woman she saw fleeing the building when they'd first arrived, but could hardly ask the question. She paused for a moment in the main foyer whilst Jean and Betty went to join Tanya outside, to collect a map of the town and a couple of leaflets from a stand on the welcome desk, her ears perking up when a small, quick-footed man entered from the back of the area and began talking to the receptionist.

"Ah, Hailey, si belle as always. When will you grants me that little soiree that I've been wanting, eh?"

"Go away, Pierre, I've told you I'm seeing someone else."

"Pah, you know we are meants to be, you and me, toi et moi. I have been telling you so since we were both here working for old Monsieur Hampton, have I nots?"

Flora didn't like to turn fully in their direction, but from the corner of her eye she thought she saw the man lean over the welcome desk, grab Hailey's hand and try to kiss it. The receptionist herself let out a grunt of disgust and quickly wheeled her chair backwards, putting herself out of the short man's reach.

Feeling uncomfortable and a bit like a voyeur to an awkward situation, Flora rushed after her friends, the warmth hitting her like a blanket the moment she stepped outside.

They opted to walk along the lane past the Crow's Nest Inn, across the wide, stone bridge and into the town square, a stroll which took less that twenty minutes, but which by the end had Flora sweating profusely. Her sunglasses kept slipping off her nose, her Italian leather sandals were pinching her toes – *had her feet actually expanded since living in Baker's Rise?* – and the indignant squawks from Reggie's carrier had become so loud, that passers-by had been assailed by rude comments for almost the whole journey. Had she not been so hot and bothered, Flora might have found it amusing when those unfortunate enough to have been 'greeted' by her pet bird looked to the sky and the trees for the origin of their abuse. It was less funny, however, when they reached the busy town square with its ornate fountain, and people started giving Flora and her group angry looks, as if they were the source of the tirade. In the end, Flora freed her rather angry parrot from what he considered his prison, endured his ensuing verbal abuse, and allowed him to travel on her shoulder. They had planned to follow the map she had picked up in the hotel lobby by walking up the ancient, cobbled street of Cobble Wynd, looping around by the old church, and then walking back down past the school in a circle. However, even Jean was flagging by the time the small group reached the bottom corner of the cobbled area, and they paused outside a grand, Victorian building.

"Bea's Book Nook – offering teas, coffees and homemade cakes in our cosy corner, that sounds grand," Betty read the sign in the window, while Flora focused on Reggie who was now circling their heads excitedly.

"Desist, silly bird," Tanya snapped, protecting her pristine curls with her handbag.

"It's the seagulls, he must want to play," Jean said sagely, commenting on the flock of birds that had appeared from the direction of the park and promenade.

"Aye well, best we get indoors quick then," Betty

replied, leading the way into the bookshop without waiting for further agreement.

"Are animals even allowed?" Flora asked belatedly, though her words were lost as the group tramped in.

"Yes, and well-behaved owners," a petite woman behind the wooden counter smiled and Flora returned the expression gratefully.

"Perfect, thank you," Flora followed her friends in, with Reggie thankfully acting the part of a perfectly behaved bird, sitting proudly on her shoulder.

"Welcome to the tearoom!" he squawked happily when they reached the back of the long room, finding an assortment of old leather couches and chairs dotted around a few antique tables. Luckily, there was a spare table, as Flora could only imagine what Betty would've had to say if there wasn't!

"Well aren't you clever," the woman from the counter, who had followed them through, spoke softly to Reggie.

"You sexy beast!" the parrot replied happily, stretching out to his full height and puffing out his little chest.

"Reginald Parrot!" Flora exclaimed in embarrassment, though the shopkeeper giggled and stroked the bird's head gently.

"Pleased to meet you, I'm Abigail, the owner of the place, but everyone calls me Bea." It was only then that Flora noticed the baby swaddled to the lady's chest in a fabric sling. Seeing the direction of her gaze, Bea added, "I'm supposed to be on maternity leave, but I'm just covering over lunchtimes."

"How old is the wee babby?" Betty asked from where she was comfortably ensconced on a squishy leather armchair.

"Just under four months, meet Daisy Mae," the woman beamed and gently pulled the fabric away from the back of the baby's head to show her cherubic face, smooth in sleep.

"She's gorgeous," Tanya declared, rather loudly and garnering an equally loud 'shh' from Betty. "Just beautiful," she whispered and they all agreed.

"I'm very proud to say she's my goddaughter and namesake," a woman who had previously had her back to them turned from her chair beside the unlit fireplace, "pleased to meet you, I'm Daisy Bloom. Are you ladies just visiting the town?"

"Daisy Bloom!" Flora exclaimed, again rather loudly,

before whispering, "Our own vicar's wife, Sally, said we should come to call on you at the vicarage."

"Well, no need, as I'm right here!" the woman, who looked to be in her mid-thirties and wore a dark denim dress adorned with a dog collar stood to greet them, garnering her a scowl from the rather prim and proper woman who was sitting opposite her. Ignoring her companion, she beamed broadly at them and said, "Do you mean the lovely Sally Marshall?"

"The very same," Betty replied, "now where's this tea and cake?"

"Ah, a lady who has her priorities in order, I see," Daisy joked and they all laughed.

"You could say that," Flora replied, somewhat sardonically, grateful for the cool room, lined with old bookshelves and the comfort of the settee whose springs seemed to have given up over the years and now afforded a very giving seat.

Yes, she thought to herself contentedly, *I could happily rest here for a few hours.*

FOUR

Unfortunately, Flora's moment of calm repose was interrupted a few short minutes later, when Bea came to take their order and rather regrettably informed the group that there were no homemade cakes at the moment, just those bought from the local bakery. As Betty made her displeasure evident, tut-tutting and muttering to Jean under her breath about false advertising, Flora felt awful. She could only imagine how the young woman in front of them must feel.

"Any scones you have will be lovely," Flora was quick to reassure Bea.

"I'm so sorry, but the girl I hired to cover my maternity leave doesn't bake, and well, as you can see I have my hands full, but the bakery scones are really lovely," the last was directed at Betty, and Flora was glad to see that her new acquaintance was not cowed by the somewhat formidable older woman.

"Aye," Jean agreed, "with a wee bit of jam and cream, that'll go down a treat!"

"Perfect," Bea moved to the serving area behind them – where everything was housed in a rather splendid wooden cabinet – to prepare the drinks, and Vicar Daisy turned once again to speak to them.

"Perhaps we could join you ladies?" she asked, the hope evident in her voice, "I think Mrs. Glendinning and I have said all we need to say to each other for now."

Sensing the tense undercurrent between the reverend and her companion, who scowled at the vicar and then directed her haughty gaze at the whole group of them, Flora swiftly responded in the positive, "Of course, we would love to hear all about the town, places to visit…"

"Cake shops and wool shops," Betty interjected, and Flora simply raised her eyebrows at Daisy, who returned the expression, a small smile on her lips.

"Well, I don't have time to be chit-chatting," the

woman opposite Daisy stood abruptly, "I have my speech for the parish council to write."

"But you will think on what I've said?" Daisy asked hopefully, "You must understand, Violet, that in order for the town to thrive we need newcomers, investment and different ventures."

"I must not understand any such thing," Violet Glendinning retorted, her voice rising to an uncomfortably high, squeaky pitch, and her hands going to her hips below her smart blazer, "My family have lived in this town for over one hundred and fifty years, and we have always encouraged the local way of life, where those who belong here own the town. Old Mr. Hampton selling the Bayview Hotel to those foreigners was the final straw! My Anthony could have bought him out! We need local byelaws in place to prevent this from happening again…"

"Isn't Anthony on his fourth trip backpacking the world, having just finished his third degree?" Daisy asked pointedly, making clear that the woman's adult son was what could politely be referred to as a 'professional student'. *No doubt with the debts to match his lack of responsibility,* Flora thought harshly, having met several such men when she was living in London.

"Well, I mean…" the woman's eyes squinted into thin

slits, as tightly closed as her mouth was open. As if she simply couldn't believe she had been spoken to like that. She quickly rallied to add, "as you well know my husband is the bank manager here at the Lillymouth branch, and he told me on good authority that they are behind with their mortgage payments already! Now, you tell me that would have happened if a local had bought the place – of course it wouldn't!"

"Violet, you shouldn't be divulging such confidential information, and neither should Percy," Daisy replied, aghast.

Violet Glendinning didn't take well to being contradicted or, even worse, chastised. With a final glare at all assembled, she manoeuvred her tall, thin frame between the seats and stalked off towards the front of the shop.

"Sorry about that," Daisy said, moving her chair closer to their table, "Violet can be rather, ah, highly strung. Perhaps it's best to forget those accusations she made about finances, never does to get involved in others' affairs, eh?"

Flora smiled and nodded, seeing that Daisy had the same tact that Sally had in Baker's Rise. She imagined the reverend would like to say a whole lot more about the memorable Mrs. Glendinning were she not in the position of parish incumbent, but instead Daisy turned the conversation to their trip. Sensing her attention on the group, Reggie flew across to the vicar's lap and made himself at home, leaving Flora praying that her little friend would button his beak or else only say phrases that were suitable for the clergy's ears!

After enjoying a peaceful hour in the cool of the bookshop, and accepting Daisy's open invitation to lunch at the vicarage later in the week, Flora was hit by the wall of heat as they ventured outside once again.

"Perhaps it would be cooler down by the bay?" Jean suggested, eying Reggie who was already flying in that direction. Flora was loathe to put the bird back in his carrier in this weather, but she was also afraid of losing him in the unfamiliar terrain or having him get himself into bother.

"I hope so," Flora replied, and the four women set off in that direction, walking along the cobbled Front Street until they reached the promenade. Despite it still being school holiday season, the area wasn't as crowded as Flora had expected. She wondered if perhaps tourists favoured the ever-popular Whitby just along the coast, with the historic abbey and its ties to Bram Stoker's 'Dracula'. Not that she was complaining

– the fewer other holidaymakers the better, as far as Flora was concerned.

"Aye, this looks nice," Betty joined the women on a wooden bench overlooking the sea, little Tina hoisted onto her lap as usual.

Following her line of sight, Flora saw that her friend was eying up a small café down on the edge of the beach, and wondered for a moment if this holiday would simply be a tour of all the coffee shops in the area – a bit of a busman's holiday for her, if she was honest. For a moment, Flora's mind went to Adam and thoughts of how different it would be if he were here now, and this were really their honeymoon. She understood, of course, that he needed time to grieve his brother and colleague, and from his rather sporadic calls and texts it seemed that the trip to the highlands of Scotland was affording him the space to do that, but still Flora's own heart lurched a little at the thought of what had happened, and what might have been.

Shaking slightly to rid herself of the unhelpful thoughts – which up till now Flora had managed to store away in a box in her head labelled 'do not open until back in Baker's Rise' – Flora stood and said, "It's hot walking, but it's absolutely baking just sitting here. I can't believe there's so little breeze – especially at this time in the afternoon! I think I'll just take a stroll along the promenade."

"I'll come with you," Tanya jumped up eagerly, as Betty launched into a detailed description of her latest crochet project.

"Aye, you young'uns have a walk down to that little coffee shop and report back on the cake situation," Betty only briefly gave them her attention before turning back to Jean, to whom Flora gave an apologetic shake of the head, "and take your bird afore he does himself a mischief!"

Realising she had not been focused on Reggie at all since she sat down, Flora's head immediately swivelled in the direction Betty indicated, watching the small green speck who was currently way down on the beach, sitting on another family's picnic blanket. The waving arms of two adults, and the excited squeals of children told Flora all she needed to know about her cheeky bird's antics.

"Oh my!" Flora exclaimed, breaking into a hop-skip-run that she knew must look comical, but the discomfort in her feet had risen to levels of real pain now, and anything other than walking very slowly put pressure on the blisters that she was sure must be forming.

Quickly overtaken by her friend, despite the woman's three-inch high, wedge heeled sandals, Flora watched as Tanya ran down the steps onto the sand, shouting, "Desist silly bird!" and apologising to the family as she went.

Take a deep breath, Flora reminded herself, as once again her little companion had caused all eyes to be on them. *It's a shame I don't enjoy being in the limelight as much as Reggie, else we could have set up a show at the end of the pier and charged for tickets,* she thought sardonically, as the squawking bundle was returned to her by a decidedly flustered Tanya, sandwich crumbs stuck to his face feathers and half a cheesy puff hanging from his beak.

FIVE

With the feathery bundle contained back in his carrier – which had been carefully placed in the shade under the bench – and after a large guzzle of water from a Tupperware box which the bird was disgusted to realise he had to share with his canine friend, Flora and Tanya finally set off for a stroll. Shrieks of "There'll be hell to pay!" followed in their wake, but Flora deliberately chose to tune Reggie out, instead focusing on the beautiful views and the hope of a moment's peace. Tanya seemed to share her sentiment, refraining from conversation and happy to walk in comfortable silence. The two women ventured along the promenade a little way, and then were tempted by the promise of shade which lured them into the large town park, mostly empty since everyone else seemed to be drawn to the beach on such a sunny day.

Following the tree-lined path and finally feeling free to remove her sun hat and wipe her sweaty brow, Flora was just about to suggest they take a look at the old Victorian bandstand which stood dead ahead, when Tanya stilled her with a hand on her elbow.

"Do you hear that?" Tanya asked in a stage whisper.

Flora didn't have to listen too intently to hear the distinctive low timbre of a man's voice, his tone clipped and angry, "We shouldn't eavesdrop," she replied, though neither woman chose to move from their spot, which was hidden from view of the people who were clearly having a heated discussion.

"I have told you, mother, you should put your foot down, ja? Don't let him boss you around. Or I will tell him, shall I? Tell him to pack his bags! You can do the cooking, ja? Goodness knows, we could do with saving the money. I was up painting bedrooms at seven this morning again to save the decorators' costs."

"Stop, Lars, I am in charge there not you. We agreed – you stay in the background and look after the accounts and I focus on the day-to-day running of the place. I haven't asked you to do any decorating, we will just do

it as we go along from the income we generate...
though how the funds ran out so quickly is beyond me.
Did you speak with the bank manager like you said
you would?"

"Then why don't you show it? Show you are in charge,
ja?" The man ignored the rest of her question, as if the
woman hadn't said it, "Instead, you come crying to me
that he has had another meltdown about you taking
ingredients from the kitchen for your baking class, and
instead of telling him not to speak to you like that and
giving him his marching orders, you flee the building!
It's a good job the customers for this afternoon's class
cancelled at the last minute. You were too soft keeping
him on when you bought the place, his food clearly
wasn't attracting guests. This would not have
happened if Father was alive. We would have the
golfing retreat in the country that he always wanted."

"Enough Lars! Your father is gone, and as you well
know it was his life insurance policy that allowed me
to fulfil this lifelong dream to own a hotel by the sea.
My dream. If he was alive, it would never have
happened – either his dream or mine – he would never
have left his precious university lecture halls and
college dinners."

"Yes, and you would still be living in Oxford having

lunch with your friends and running charity galas for the local hospice," the man said bitterly.

Flora suspected this may be the woman she had seen running from the hotel earlier, but didn't dare walk any further to confirm it. Instead, she and Tanya listened in silence, feeling only slightly guilty for doing so. *What is it about hearing the trials in others' lives that makes us feel better about our own?*

"Is that all you think I'm good for?" The woman asked, a distinct hitch in her voice, "I mean, I'm sixty-five not ninety!"

"Of course not, mother, I simply think you may have bitten off more than you can chew. Now, if you would let me take over full management of the place, and you stick to your cakes, I could…"

"No, Lars!" Her voice was firmer now, and Flora silently cheered the stranger on, "No. This is my dream, you must find your own. Even if it turns into a nightmare, I'll see it through!"

One of the speakers must have turned their back to them, or walked off entirely, for that was the last Flora and Tanya heard of the conversation.

"Well, that was interesting," Tanya said, as they

themselves pivoted to walk back in the direction they had come, "do you think they were talking about our hotel?"

"I'm not sure. Probably, though, as when I originally looked to book somewhere in the town there was only one other hotel, the local inn and several B&B's to choose from, besides..." Flora went on to explain about the woman she had seen hurrying from the back door of their hotel earlier.

"Well, I wonder if there'll be any excitement at dinner?" Tanya said, not even trying to hide the hope in her voice.

"You mean other than Betty complaining about the effect of the heat on her bunions?" Flora joked, linking arms with her friend and happily breathing in a lungful of salty sea air.

After lukewarm showers from rattling pipes – which were welcome in the heat but would have been awful in the winter – Flora and her friends faced the not-so-small dilemma of what to do with the animals whilst they were at dinner. The evening meal came as part of the holiday package, so Flora really didn't fancy the prospect of taking turns to miss it in order that someone could look after the pets. Nor, however, were they allowed to accompany the women into the dining room – the surly-faced girl on the desk had made that quite clear when, as they made their hot and sweaty return to the hotel, the group had enquired as to where and when the meal would take place. Hailey had given a long and unwavering warning glare in Tina's direction as she spoke, which Flora correctly interpreted as the animals must also be kept well away from the reception area.

Too tired then to argue, Flora and Betty had come down now to resume the conversation, though Flora had to admit she felt only slightly more refreshed. Other than their own, which still smelled of fresh paint, the upstairs rooms were clearly still waiting for the makeover which the downstairs of the hotel had undergone. The wallpaper was peeling in places in the hallways, the carpets were frayed at the edges and the bath ware in their suite had clearly not been replaced for years. On top of which, one shower for four grown women was not exactly ideal. Flora took a slow, deep breath in and out, repeating it whilst Betty stated their case yet again.

Since she hadn't envisaged bringing Reggie on this trip, Flora did feel slightly galled now that she was having to try to make arrangements for him and was inclined to let her friend do all the persuading.

"As I said before," Hailey didn't even try to hide the exasperation from her voice, "the only option you have is to stay with them in the room, or place them in the laundry room, where they must remain overnight anyway."

"You're looking nice," Betty said, as Hailey looked around for a menu to show the women, perhaps hoping the distraction of food would stop them asking about the animals, "all fancy like. Going courting tonight?"

"Betty!" Flora said aghast. *Was her friend determined to make the receptionist dislike them even more? Or was she trying to butter her up to give their pets special privileges?*

"Aye well, she looks all dolled up, doesn't she?"

"Actually I do have a date, yes," Hailey replied smugly, flicking her hair – released from the severe bun of earlier and now cascading down her back – and jutting out her chest, of which rather a lot was visible, her top being as low cut as it was. She had shed the receptionist's uniform in favour of a rather more… sultry outfit.

Flora followed the young woman's gaze out of the big

bay window to where a smartly dressed man, in his mid-thirties maybe, was speaking with an older gent on a sit-on lawnmower, his hands gesticulating back towards the main building. She wondered briefly if either could have been the male voice that she and Tanya had heard that afternoon. The older man looked out of the age range to have been talking to his mother, but the younger was a definite possibility. Flora wasn't even sure why she cared, other than her usual curiosity getting the better of her! *What's more, could the younger of the two be Hailey's date for the evening? He's certainly older than her, but I've seen stranger matches…* Flora's mind continued its pondering as she tuned out of the conversation next to her. Betty was currently quizzing the poor receptionist on whether the choux pastry for the steak and ale pie had been made using the traditional method, and it was too late in a tiring day for Flora to have any hope of reining her friend in. Instead, she stood watching the two men outside, filled with a sudden urge to speak to her own fiancé.

Despite not marrying the previous week, the couple had agreed to stay engaged. They definitely wanted to be joined as man and wife, just in a quieter, more private way than the whole bells-and-whistles celebration that had been arranged at The Rise. Pushing away the knowledge that she should give him space and focus on her own time away, Flora excused herself and found a quiet spot in a corner of the hotel lounge to call Adam. The reception and seating areas were one large, open space and had clearly been recently decorated in a Scandinavian style – the exposed floorboards had been sanded and whitewashed, and were adorned by cosy cream rugs, a contrast to the green foliage that was dotted all around the space.

Flora found the soft hues of the décor calming – *hygge, isn't that what it's called?* She wondered as she moved a throw blanket and some cushions, in order to feel the cool wood of the back of the sofa against her – it was still too hot, even this late in the day, to want to be cosied up with home furnishings.

"Flora?" Adam answered after the fourth ring.

"Adam? Hi!"

"Hello love, you're lucky you got hold of me, the reception up here is something terrible. Good for getting away from everything though."

Flora's own insecurity made her worry that that was a dig at her for making the call, but she pushed it aside to worry about later and ploughed on, "That was good timing then. How… ah, how are things?" Now that they were actually speaking, she stumbled over what would be the right thing to say. They were far apart in physical distance, but right now the emotional one felt pretty insurmountable too. Adam had left straight after their friends' joint wedding and they hadn't spoken properly since – Flora hadn't realised how much she needed to feel close to him again until right now.

"Good, good. Are you calling because something's happened? Did you get there safely?"

"Oh yes, I mean no, nothing's up, yes we got here safely, though it's very hot and the animals ended up coming with us... Adam? Adam?"

Presented with the dial tone again, Flora tried to call back, but each time it went straight to voicemail. It was the bad reception, she was sure. Of course it was. He would want to have a quick chat.

Wouldn't he?

It was a decidedly snappy Flora who interrupted Betty's rather one-sided conversation with the receptionist, whose eyes were now flashing daggers at them both.

"I was just saying..." her friend began, but Flora's last

shred of patience was gone for the day.

"Now, Betty, let's get the others and go for dinner. We'll shut the animals in wherever they show us."

To her own credit, Betty didn't bite back. She simply looked at the mobile phone which was still clasped in Flora's hand, her knuckles white from the grip, raised her eyebrows in silent question and rubbed Flora's shoulder in a maternal way.

"Come on then lass."

To be honest, Flora wanted nothing more in that moment than a big hug, but her emotional walls were up, and she only had herself to blame for not asking for one.

SIX

Despite the laundry room being along a small corridor that led past the kitchens, and then down a short, steep set of stairs, Flora found the walk into a cooler part of the old building refreshing. Indeed, when the young lad – who looked to be a waiter – who had guided her there scuttled off quickly, leaving Flora to return to the dining room alone, she took her time getting the animals settled. A moment even half to herself was a most welcome thought right now!

Speaking in hushed, reassuring tones, Flora was glad when Tina snuggled down in the washing basket that had been provided. No doubt the little dog was exhausted from their busy day – to be honest, Flora felt quite jealous and could easily have curled up somewhere cosy herself at this point.

Reggie, as you can imagine, was not so easily settled. Even as Flora tried to mollify him with a banana she had taken from the bowl of complimentary fruit in the honeymoon suite, he refused to leave her shoulder, his pointy talons gripping her to the point of pain.

"Now, Reginald Parrot, I don't have the time or the energy for this," Flora scolded, crouching down and trying to tip the bird onto a wooden clothes horse which would serve as a makeshift perch.

"You silly old trout!" the bird responded, clinging on until Flora was at such an angle that her back cracked worryingly and finally the parrot was forced to relinquish his grip.

"Really!" Flora exclaimed, leaving the banana slices next to the seeds, dog food and water which she had already arranged, and rushing to the door, eager to get out lest the clingy bird fly straight back to her.

Closing the door firmly and leaning her back against the cool wood, Flora took several deep breaths. Ear piercing screeches and squawks of "Bad bird!" could be heard from the other side, but Flora straightened up and chose to ignore the racket. Rubbing the base of her spine in slow circles, she made her way gingerly up the small staircase and onto the corridor that was normally reserved for staff only. It was as she was approaching the kitchen on her right that Flora heard raised voices for the second time that day. A woman's voice, which was similar if not identical to the one from the park, and a man's heavily European accent – *French*, Flora thought to herself, *same as the man coming on to Hailey in reception earlier* – and she couldn't help but pause before reaching the door to that room. Yet again she found herself eavesdropping – *it must be the day for it*, Flora thought, only feeling slightly guilty.

"Zut alors, Ingrid! I will not be accepting zis! I needs the moneys to buy the foods!"

"It's Mrs. Hansen to you. And, as I have told you Pierre, with the decorating costs and the time it's taking to build up a regular clientele again, you'll have to accept the budget I've given you. We all know the state the place was left in when I took over." Now, that was something Flora understood all too well. The refurbishment of her own manor house at The Rise had been a black hole which seemed to inhale funds.

"Pah! I could do ze better jobs myself! And I'm an artiste, a creative artiste, you are stifling ze muse!"

"Excuse me, Pierre, I am the owner here and if you aren't happy, well then the door is right there!" Flora silently applauded the woman who had obviously taken her son's advice from earlier, though the shake in the speaker's voice was unmistakable. Disliking confrontation herself, Flora could completely sympathise.

As footsteps approached, Flora took off along the corridor again, faster this time, and entered the airy dining room where her friends were seated around a circular table in the large bay window overlooking the North sea. This room had also been decorated in soft creams and whites, with pristine cotton tablecloths and candle-filled lanterns on each table. It was a shame there were no other diners here to appreciate it.

"Did my Tina settle?" Betty asked, taking a sip of what looked to be sherry in a dainty, cut crystal glass.

"Yes, straight away… unfortunately the same can't be said for Reggie," Flora accepted the glass of red which Tanya gestured to and took a grateful sip, "at least we can't hear him from up here."

"Aye, let's try to forget about them and enjoy the meal," Jean smiled, passing Flora a menu.

"Here here," Tanya agreed, adjusting the sparkling tiara which she was wearing to match the sequined mini dress she had changed into for the evening. Flora felt rather dowdy in comparison, in her floral linen dress, though she was cool and comfortable for perhaps the first time that day and would take that as a win.

"Now, let's see if the soup in the list of starters is actually homemade with fresh garden produce," Betty said, rubbing her hands together as if she was preparing for battle.

And with that, Flora's stress returned.

It was when Betty had sent her third note of the meal to the chef – via the shy waiter from earlier – messages which Flora knew certainly couldn't be interpreted as compliments, that the man himself appeared with the woman that Flora had seen fleeing the building when they arrived.

"Ladies, it's a pleasure to meet you, my name is Ingrid Hansen, and I'm the owner of the hotel," the woman had a tight smile and glanced nervously at the small, red-faced man beside her from the side of her eye, "I hope you are enjoying your meal?"

Betty scraped up the last few crumbs of her strawberry cheesecake – the third plate she had wiped clean in as many courses – and was obviously about to launch into her thoughts on the fare.

"It was lovely, thank you," Flora interjected quickly, observing the grateful look that flashed across her host's face, "as you can see, we've all cleared our plates."

"Oh, well that's good, very good," the relief in Ingrid's tone was evident.

"But, what about ze petits messages?" The man stood with his hands clasped, sweat dripping down his nose and into his pristine little moustache. Flora tried not to smile, thinking how the chef resembled the esteemed fictional detective Hercules Poirot. His flustered expression was very different from that other monsieur, though, and Flora wondered how he would look if he'd had to cook for forty and not four. And that was before she even thought about the unwanted attention he was giving the receptionist earlier, certainly not like the gentlemanly Belgian detective.

"Ah, just some ah, constructive compliments," Jean replied diplomatically, "very good meal, lovely."

The chef seemed slightly mollified by this, but just as he opened his mouth to speak once again there was a tapping at the window in front of them, and a loud,

"My Flora!" which caught everyone's attention.

"What the..?" Tanya twisted sideways to regard what Flora could clearly see from her spot opposite the window – a rather familiar little bird, flapping his wings and tapping his beak against the glass to get their attention. This was in fact one of many moments recently that Flora wished the ground would open up and swallow her.

As it was, she rose slowly from her seat, and turned to face Ingrid Hansen, "Ah, that would be my parrot."

"Parrot?" The chef asked, his high pitched voice sounding almost comical, "This is not ze zoo, Madame!"

"Ah, I did leave him in the laundry room as instructed," Flora shrugged her shoulders helplessly.

"A little Houdini, I see," Ingrid said smiling, and Flora returned the kind expression as she unhooked her handbag from the back of her chair and set off to find the source of her embarrassment and return him to the laundry.

Then there was the small question of how the bird had escaped in the first place… Flora sighed, slow and deep.

A Walk In The Parkin

This was going to be a long night.

SEVEN

Thankfully there didn't seem to be any other guests in the hotel that night to hear the little parrot who was most put out to be returned to the laundry room, where Flora quickly saw the means of his earlier escape – a sash window which had been left ajar. It took quite a lot of strength for Flora to push the old, wooden aperture down to close the gap, and she was sweating again by the time she had completed the small task. Of course, the loud bird clamped onto her shoulder didn't help matters, shrieking "Now there's trouble!" directly into her ear on repeat.

Little Tina, bless her, snored peacefully throughout the whole encounter, and Flora wondered for a brief moment why she hadn't inherited a dog instead. *Surely an animal that at least couldn't answer back would be so much... easier!* Not that she really wanted to change Reggie, of course, but in moments like this a little daydream was only natural, Flora reassured herself, as she once again rushed from the room, a definite sense of déjà-vu about the action.

Despite the heat and the unfamiliar sleeping arrangements, the four women managed a passable night and woke up refreshed the next day and mostly excited for the baking class – which is to say, Betty was desperate to get started and the others were slightly apprehensive of her exuberance.

After a hearty full English breakfast, with thankfully no sign of the rather sensitive chef and the addition of a decidedly lovely fan which had been placed by their table, Flora rushed back along the dimly lit corridor to release the captives.

"You silly old trout! Bad bird! My Flora! She's a corker! I'm all shook up!" Reggie couldn't quite decide whether he wanted to be angry with her, or to compliment Flora so much that she didn't put him back in the space later. Either way, as soon as she opened the door to retrieve them both animals rushed ahead of her back towards the kitchen before Flora could catch up with them.

"Argh!" A very feminine shriek stopped all three in their tracks, as the woman who was exiting the kitchen almost tripped over Tina by her feet. Turning to face Flora, her eyes ablaze with indignation, Hailey stood with her hands on her hips.

"What on earth are they doing here?" she asked, her breath coming in short gasps, and her skin looking decidedly flushed, which Flora thought was overly excessive for the situation – albeit regrettable – in which they now found themselves. If she wasn't mistaken, though, Flora thought she saw the imprint of a hand on the woman's cheek, which would account for some of her heightened colour and frazzled state.

"I'm retrieving them from the laundry, where you insisted I leave them for the night," Flora spoke gently, trying to keep a check on her own annoyance. *Who really knew what was going on in others' lives? Best to tread carefully and be kind,* she reminded herself.

Hailey sneezed twice and glared at Flora from above the paint-covered hands which now hovered over her nose and mouth, "Unacceptable!" she mumbled, before turning on her heel and rushing in the direction of the front desk.

Whilst the young woman was back to wearing her daytime receptionist uniform, though without the blazer – because of the heat, Flora presumed – Flora couldn't help but notice that the back of her tightly-fitting blouse was pulled out of the woman's skirt and crumpled as if someone had taken a fist full of it. She didn't have time to speculate however, nor to have a quick nosey into the kitchen to see who may or may not have also been in there, as the animals had taken off once more and Flora had the embarrassing job of keeping up with them.

After a stroll around the beautiful hotel gardens, and an extremely early elevenses of cream scones and pots of tea on the patio – which Betty insisted upon, despite them all still being full from breakfast – it was time for the baking class to begin. The cookery studio was in a large room off the reception area at the back, a beautiful, airy space with floor to ceiling windows overlooking the back patio where the women had just been sitting. The windows, and a set of French double doors, were all open slightly to let in the slight sea breeze – a very welcome addition! Ingrid herself was immaculate in an apron which bore the hotel's name and logo, and a hairnet which covered her blonde bun, held tight at the nape of her neck.

"Ah, we weren't sure what to do with..." Flora gestured almost helplessly at the terrier in Betty's arms and at the parrot on her own shoulder who was currently craning his neck and ogling the ingredients laid out on the large bench before them.

"Not to worry, I thought about your little friends, and although for hygiene reasons I can't allow them to stay in here, I'm more than happy for them to wait in my office," Ingrid led Flora and Betty to a small room off the back corner of the studio. There were two identical doors, one in each corner behind the main workbench – one, Flora presumed must be the entry to a larder or storeroom for ingredients and equipment, and this one which opened into a bright office space. It was no bigger than a large cupboard, really, but the room boasted the same full-length, original sash window and high ceiling as the main space, complete with a large whirring fan, giving it the allusion of being larger than it was. Laid out on a fluffy blanket on the floor were two water dishes, some dog treats and a small bowl of blueberries.

"She's a corker!" Reggie squawked, flying from Flora's shoulder straight down to the treats below, and causing Ingrid to blush lightly.

"Thank you so much," Flora felt almost overwhelmed

by the small gesture, and tears sprang to her eyes making her feel silly.

"Not at all, we like to welcome all our guests," Ingrid bent down to stroke Tina, kindly giving Flora time to compose herself. Betty had already left the room, no doubt to examine the ingredients laid out for them, and Flora flashed her hostess a watery smile.

"I have my own manor house and tearoom," Flora began by way of explanation, "and I know how difficult it can be to meet guests' expectations. So much to juggle and to remember. I could learn a lot from you."

"Maybe I'll visit some day," Ingrid smiled as they shut the door softly on the terrible twosome.

"You would be very welcome," Flora replied, as she took her seat on a free stool on the opposite side of the long counter to Ingrid.

Swiftly putting on the beautifully pressed apron that was waiting for her, Flora caught Jean's eye beside her, and they both raised a hopeful eyebrow in shared understanding...

If they could get through this without Betty finding fault with anything or offering them all the benefit of her own experience it would be a miracle!

EIGHT

Well that didn't last long, Flora thought sardonically, as she shared another knowing look with Jean, after Betty had asked her third question in as many minutes. Thankfully, the four of them were the only ones taking this class.

"Why did you choose that type of oatmeal? How many times have you baked this recipe? Does it come out moist every time if you leave it for a few days in the cake tin to develop? Did you know I was chairwoman of the local Women's Institute for fifteen years..?" and on she went. Ingrid had been patience personified, and Flora knew she herself would have snapped by now, but the Scandinavian answered all of Betty's questions with such calm and authority, Flora could tell this was where she was totally at home – in her own kitchen rather than juggling the demands of a hotelier's life.

In the end, Tanya interrupted on behalf of them all – to sighs of relief from Flora and Jean – and asked Betty somewhat bluntly to "shut her trap for five minutes and let the poor woman speak!" If Betty was put out by this, she barely showed it, simply donning the thick skin she so often wore in public and clicking her tongue against her teeth.

"So, ah where was I?" Ingrid asked, with a half-smile and running her hands over her scraped back hair, "The original, traditional Yorkshire parkin always contains oatmeal – any medium oatmeal is acceptable, as I advised Betty here – and without it, the cake is simply a regular gingerbread. The best parkin recipe needs to produce a bake that is moist, sticky and full of ginger. As you will taste later, proper parkin has a nutty texture coming from the medium oats, and deep toffee flavours created by the addition of dark black treacle."

"And what would you know of proper, traditional Yorkshire parkin?" The rude interruption came from the main door to the room. Spinning on her high stool, Flora recognised the rather unfriendly woman – decidedly unfriendly now, in her opinion – from the book nook yesterday. Striding into the room with two other ladies in tow, Violet Glendinning had angry eyes set on Ingrid, who visibly retreated further behind the long counter they all shared.

"Well, I don't think that is justified!" Betty piped up, before Flora herself had gotten over her shock enough to speak. Her friend may have her faults, as they all did, but she wouldn't stand by and let someone be bullied and belittled.

"What business is it of yours?" Violet snapped back, "You only arrived in the town yesterday."

"Well, I've baked German strudel, having never been to Germany. I've followed a Spanish crochet pattern having never visited Spain. Do you have glasses in your handbag, because you're certainly short-sighted! Sticking your beak where it's not wanted, you're a regular nosy parkin!" Betty added rather triumphantly, happy with her little pun.

"And narrow minded!" Tanya added, as all the Baker's Rise women nodded in agreement.

Ingrid flashed them all a grateful smile.

"Were you wanting to book onto the class, it has actually already started…" Hailey rushed in now behind the women, somewhat belatedly, looking even more flustered than earlier. Her ponytail was askew and her cheeks flushed, making Flora wonder what she could have been doing as there were no other guests to attend to. She didn't have time to ponder, however, as Violet Glendinning was far from finished with what she had come to say.

"Of course not, you silly girl, I wouldn't sit through a class taught by this foreign charlatan if it was…"

"And that's all we need to hear of that," Jean stood with surprising speed, followed swiftly by Betty. Taking an elbow each they escorted Violet from the room, her two silent partners trailing behind, their stoic expressions not having changed throughout the whole exchange.

"What the..? Well, I have never been treated…" Violet's blustering and barking faded into the distance.

"Oh, I'm sure you have!" Flora heard Betty saying, and felt like applauding, but there was no time to experience the small moment of celebration as poor Ingrid was clutching the counter top opposite her.

"Ingrid!" Flora exclaimed as she and Tanya rushed around to help the woman.

"Just hot, just hot," Ingrid whispered, as they helped her to one of the cushioned window seats that dotted the room.

"I'll fetch a glass of water," Tanya said, her wide, tie-dyed pantaloons billowing out as she hurried to the sink.

"What's all this?" the accented male voice, recognisable from the park the previous day, could be heard before the man it belonged to entered the room, "Mamma, why are you sitting there? We have guests to attend to!" He shot an angry look towards Ingrid and then tried to school his features as he indicated Flora with a sharp lift of his eyebrow.

"Ja, Lars, ja," Ingrid tried to rise, but Flora pushed her shoulder gently back down.

"We are being very well looked after, Mr. Hansen is it?" Flora graced the man with her sternest look.

"Excellent, ja, excellent," as if a switch had been flicked, the man turned on the charm, flashing his pearly whites at Flora and Tanya, who had returned with the drink. Little did he know that such charismatic tactics would have absolutely no effect on these women, who had been round the block more than once in their lives.

"Your... mother is it? Needs some rest. It is no fault of hers that the local Moaning Minnie brigade showed up here," Flora said, as Betty and Jean re-joined the group.

"Yes, this is my son, Lars," Ingrid said feebly, and Flora hated the way her new friend almost cowered in his presence, "he, ah, helps me run the place."

"Yes well, let's get you off to bed, mother. We'll discuss this later."

Determined that he wouldn't speak to Ingrid as if she were a child, Flora spoke up once more to add, "Actually, I think some fresh air and a cup of sweet tea on the patio would serve your mother much better than a stifling hot bedroom right now." Ignoring the man's scowl, Tanya and Flora helped Ingrid gently to her feet, happy to see that the colour was returning to her cheeks.

"Aye and we'll have some scones and parkin with that," Betty gave the shocked man their order as the five women left him standing.

"I'll just get the animals," Flora said, when the others were all happily seated under a parasol on the patio in the shade of the building.

Well, that could've gone better, she thought to herself as she hurried back inside the building through the side door, *I bet Reverend Daisy has her hands full with that lot!*

NINE

"Thank you again, ladies, a good chat was exactly what I needed," a much more relaxed Ingrid expressed her gratitude for the second time, "I will of course make sure the class and all of the refreshments are removed from your bill. Perhaps you would be willing to try again tomorrow?"

"Of course," Betty answered for the group, causing Flora to smile widely at her friend, "and you heed my word, ignore those others, they're probably just jealous of your baking skills – something I've had to deal with a lot over the years…"

"Anyway…" Jean interjected quickly.

"Well then, if you'll excuse me, I need to clear up the baking bench and then I think I'll go and work in my office. The fan in there keeps it nice and cool, and I can often hide away for hours if I'm lucky!" Ingrid stood and brushed scone crumbs from her apron. The statement was rather telling, Flora thought, and – not for the first time – she felt sympathy towards the woman.

After sitting for another half an hour or so, the group decided to take a stroll down to the harbour for a fish and chips lunch at Betty's suggestion. The women gathered up their things, donned their sunhats and were about to leave with their pets in tow, when Betty started hunting around under the table.

"Where is it, Tina?"

"Where's what?" Flora's back protested as she bent down to look underneath the table, where Reggie and Tina were still munching on an assortment of crumbs which Betty must've been secretly passing them whilst the women were talking.

"Tina's lead, the stripey one."

"Oh, I took it off her when I left them in the office there, have you had it since?" Flora asked, dabbing the sweat that had already started running down her brow at the slight movement.

"Ah, that'll be it then, I'll just pop and get it, here you take Tina for a minute," and with that Betty hurried off, clutching her handbag to her chest, "you just go on slowly, I'll catch up!"

"Has Betty still not caught up to us?" Flora looked behind her worriedly, the little bird on her shoulder picking up on the sudden tension in her shoulders and neck and taking off to hover above them.

"Secrets and lies!" he shrieked, garnering them more than a couple of enquiring glances from the groups sitting outside the Crow's Nest Inn on garden tables, pints in hand. Flora felt a stab of guilt that they had already reached this point, without wondering where Betty was – it was a good five minute walk from the hotel, even at Tanya's quick pace.

"I was just wondering that," Jean replied, "I keep looking behind us, but no sight of her."

"One of us should go back," Flora said decisively, the all-too-familiar lurch in her gut telling her that something was not right.

"We'll all go," Tanya said, putting an arm around

Flora's shoulders, "we are in no rush to get anywhere, let's find Betty and set back out together."

"Agreed," Jean said, though even she had a worried expression, further fuelling Flora's own concerns. As was often the case, she couldn't put her finger on what exactly it was that had happened, just that something felt 'off'.

"You get the bad feeling again? Unsettled?" Tanya asked softly, as the three women, a parrot and a dog, hurried back down Crow's Nest Lane to the hotel.

"How did you know?" Flora asked, somewhat surprised by her friend's intuition.

"My grandmother in Ukraine had the same gut feelings – exact same look she got too – and was what people would now call an empath. Back then, people thought she must just be a busybody. Anyway, I see the same with you. It is both a blessing and a curse, no?"

"It really is," Flora replied, hoping to goodness that it was simply a case of Betty having succumbed to the lure of more tea and cakes at the hotel. Deep down, though, she knew this wouldn't be the case.

There was no one at the reception desk when the women rushed in. Not that Hailey's absence was ominous, as she didn't seem to have been really focused on her job earlier in the day either. What was worrying, however, desperately so, was the keening scream that came from the direction of the baking studio.

Hurrying forwards, and trying to ignore the piercing shriek of the parrot above her, who echoed the noise coming from the baking studio with his own prediction of "There'll be hell to pay," Flora stopped short behind Hailey, who seemed to be frozen just inside the doorway of the room and was the source of all the noise.

"Tanya, would you mind keeping the animals out here in reception?" Jean asked sagely.

"Of course," Flora heard Tanya reply from behind her as she turned to face the receptionist and shooed Reggie off her shoulder.

"Hailey, what is it?"

The woman sneezed twice, causing Flora to almost lose her temper with impatience and to repeat, "Hailey!"

"Over there, it's…. she's covered in blood and…"

Flora didn't wait to hear the rest of the halting sentence, peppered as it was with sobs. Hurrying behind the baking counter in the direction of the office and leaving Jean to talk some sense out of the girl, Flora was met with Betty, slumped on the floor and covered in what looked distinctly like blood. Her friend's eyes were staring blankly and her face a clammy shade of pale.

"Betty! Betty, no!" Flora dropped to her knees on the hard floor, taking in the horror of the view before her, "Betty, please!" Flora could hear the high pitch of her plea – a shriek really, and spent an awful moment mourning her friend, imagining the conversation she would have with Harry, the hole that would be left in both of their lives...

"Aye lass, help me up would you? There'll be time for tears when I'm actually dead!"

"Betty?" The relief which flooded Flora as she helped her friend to her feet was like a balm to her frazzled soul, "But you're covered in..?"

"Blood. Aye, but not mine lass... I tried to save her, Flora, I..." and Betty's own voice cracked and she slumped into Flora's arms, sobbing uncontrollably.

"Here, let me take her, I've told that young receptionist

to phone the police," Jean spoke quickly.

"Thank you, and I'll go and look in the office," Flora spoke slowly, the dread of what she was about to find already replacing the relief in her body tenfold.

"Are you sure? We could wait and…"

"No, I'll see if there's anything I can do," Flora replied.

"Just don't touch anything," Jean advised, rather ominously, though Flora agreed and frankly had no intention of having more than a quick peek.

Given the amount of blood that covered Betty, Flora had an idea of the scene that was about to greet her, and nausea settled in her throat just thinking about it.

Nevertheless, face it she must.

TEN

Flora sat on one of the cushioned window seats, her back bent and her head between her knees as she waited for the world to stop spinning. A mixing bowl sat on the floor beside her, ready for any further evacuation of the contents of her stomach. To say the scene that greeted her in the small office off the baking studio had been horrific would be an understatement and, other than checking for a pulse and finding none, Flora had not spent a second more than necessary in the space.

As she bent her head to check for life, however, and trying to avert her eyes from the worst of it, Flora had caught sight of a large, blood-splattered kitchen knife under the now-open window.

Whoever did this to poor Ingrid must be either a fool or they were almost caught in the act, probably by our poor Betty, Flora had thought to herself, as Jean led her away from the scene of carnage.

Not that it was her place to speculate. All that Flora cared about was getting her own light-headedness under control so that she could help her friend, who sat shaking beside her.

"I have put the animals back in the laundry room," Tanya explained, hurrying towards them, "that silly girl is on the phone to the police, but goodness knows whether they can understand her, because she is still crying and shrieking."

"She didn't even go into the office with the… the body, just saw me covered in blood from the doorway there and started screaming," Betty whispered, "she's probably telling them I'm dead."

"Well, as long as the police come, I'm sure it'll all become clear when they get here," Jean replied, the voice of reason as always, "Now, shall I phone Harry to drive down here? I think it might be for the best."

"What? No. No need to worry the man," Betty said emphatically, shaking her head and making her grey curls bob frantically up and down, "I just need to get cleaned up and have a cup of Earl Grey to restore my constituency."

"Your constitution, yes I'll see if there's a kettle over there," Jean said kindly, sharing a look with Tanya.

"Is my little Tina okay?" Betty asked, the wobble back in her voice.

"Well, the window was open, but I shut it so we shouldn't have little escape artists like last night," Tanya tried but failed to smile.

"Strange, I shut that window last night, and since we're the only guests, it's unlikely they have much laundry this early in the day…" Flora mused, her head whirring. She could only imagine the cacophony of noise her little parrot was making at being incarcerated again so soon.

"I tried to save her, you know," Betty's voice was merely a whisper now, "but it was too much… there was too much…"

"It's okay Betty, we know," Flora was sitting up straight now, her arm around Betty's trembling shoulders.

"What's all this?" The low baritone of Lars' voice filtered over to them from the doorway. Apparently,

Hailey hadn't thought to call for the man, nor had she been in reception to update him, as Ingrid's son stalked over to them, "My God, what has happened? Are you okay? We have liability insurance if you're thinking of making a claim."

"A claim?" Tanya asked, somewhat incredulous that this was the first thing the man would think of.

"I'm not hurt, lad," Betty looked at him with wide, shocked eyes, "It's... I'm so sorry, it's your mother."

"My mother? I told her to lie down. If only she would listen. I'll speak to her..." and with that he strode off again, leaving the women shaking their heads in sympathy for what he would find.

"Ah, I wouldn't go in there," Jean began, but it was too late. Lars was too focused on reaching his mother's office to heed her advice.

The next hour passed in a blur of sirens, of loud footsteps and even louder questions. Flora's head throbbed with it all, especially since they had been told not to leave the room. Poor Betty had not even been allowed to clean up and change her dress. In fact, she had been the focus of the detectives' attention for the majority of the time since they arrived. Detective Inspector Matlock was a stocky woman, with an unforgiving glare and a distinct air that you were guilty until proven innocent. She directed her team with a series of brief, clipped orders, which they must surely be used to following because at times Flora couldn't understand what the woman was asking them to do. She took aloof and haughty to a whole new level, one not even the late departed Detective Blackett had managed to achieve.

Flora wiped a lone tear from her cheek, and wished desperately – and not for the first time – that Adam was here. Or, at least in Baker's Rise where she could contact him, rather than in the wilds of the highlands.

"So, you others are not to leave the hotel, we will come to take a formal statement later today," Flora suddenly snapped out of her own internal musings to realise that a uniformed officer was leading Betty away from the opposite corner of the large room, where a table and chairs had been set up for interviewing purposes, and that the lead detective was addressing the three of them.

"No, I mean yes, but no, you can't take Betty," Flora stood as she spoke, as if to emphasize her point, as Betty shouted, "Look after my Tina!" in a half sob from across the room.

"Mrs. Bentley is coming to the station to help us with our enquiries," Matlock spoke without emotion, though the disdainful look she bestowed on Flora spoke a thousand words, "you shall all remain here in the hotel and we will interview you again in due course, as we work through the staff."

"But, we told you about Mrs. Glendinning and her protest," Jean stood shoulder to shoulder with Flora.

"You did," the detective said simply, before turning and giving them her back.

"Well!" Tanya exclaimed, clearly ready to say more on the matter, but Jean shook her head at her, silently advising caution.

The three women sat back down forlornly on the chairs that had been placed next to the window seat, and Jean whispered, "I'll phone Harry, he would want to know. There's nothing else we can do but wait. Finding Betty covered in the victim's blood was obviously going to, ah, raise questions."

"I'll take you back to your room," Hailey appeared ten minutes later, with a police officer in tow. Clearly agitated, her eyes swollen and red, she gripped the hem of her shirt which seemed to swamp her curvy figure and crumpled it between her white-knuckled grasp.

"What about my bird and my friend's dog?" Flora spoke up sharply, "They cannot stay contained all day."

"Yes, ah, whatever you like, take them to your room," Hailey shrugged her shoulders as if she had given up caring, and the three women trailed her out, the police officer taking up position behind them.

ELEVEN

"Bad Bird! Bad bird! Now there's trouble!"

Flora could hear the angry squawks before she had even passed the kitchen, noting that the room itself had been cordoned off by yellow police tape, no doubt because they had found the kitchen knife near the murder victim.

"Pipe down!" Flora responded as she approached the laundry room, using one of Reggie's own phrases.

"You pipe down! All shook up!" Came the shrieked response, accompanied by a couple of sharp barks from the room's other occupant.

Flora didn't linger, not when a murderer was on the

loose in the hotel and they needed to figure out a way to draw attention away from Betty.

Surely, Flora thought as she gathered up the animals and their belongings, *there must be plenty of suspects, why I can think of four at least.*

Adam's voice popped into her head, overriding Flora's own with words of caution and telling her in no uncertain terms not to get involved, exactly as he would if he were here now. Flora resisted the urge to pull her mobile phone from her handbag and call her fiancé, instead hurrying back the way she had come and up the main staircase to the bridal suite, trying to ignore the young policeman who had trailed her the whole way.

"Just in time, the kettle's just boiled," Jean said as Flora entered the living area, "I think we could all do with a cup of hot, sweet tea. I've phoned Harry, whatever Betty said I know she needs him here, and since he's only a few hours away it made sense to let him know as quickly as possible."

Flora was grateful for the older woman's steady head in such circumstances, and slumped into an armchair by the bay window with the mug Jean offered her. There was no sign of Tanya, and Flora was just about to ask as to her whereabouts when the bathroom door opened and her friend appeared.

"She's a corker!" Reggie squawked from his perch on the back of a chair, and Flora wasn't sure whether he was referring to Tanya's presence in general or to the teeny tiny pair of denim shorts she had changed into. Her wet hair was wrapped in a towel turban-style and for once her friend was free of her signature make up.

"I felt dirty," Tanya said simply, and Flora understood exactly what she meant. In fact, a lukewarm shower sounded very pleasant right now, what with the constant heat, and the images which kept flashing on repeat through her head…

"We'll have these refreshments and then get a taxi to the police station and see what we can do for Betty," Jean said decisively.

"Except we can't leave the hotel," Flora replied.

"Oh, I had forgotten that," Jean sounded defeated and Tanya came to put her arm around their friend's shoulders.

"We can have the drinks and then head downstairs and see what we can find out," Tanya said, bending to stroke little Tina who was circling their legs somewhat pitifully, clearly looking for her owner.

"I imagine they'll have officers stationed at the main entrance and the rooms closed off," Flora said, "but I think we'll go mad if we just sit here and do nothing."

"Mad, mad! Silly bird!" Reggie flew onto Flora's shoulder and she welcomed the softness of his downy feathers against her cheek.

"Poor Ingrid," Flora began, but no sooner were the words out of her mouth than a heavy banging interrupted their quiet chat.

"What on earth?" Tanya asked, as Reggie began squawking "Pipe down! Hide it all!" which helped nothing.

"I'll get it," Flora said, bending to pick up the little yapping bundle of tremoring terrier and handing the frightened dog to Jean, who cuddled Tina immediately into her lap.

"I'm sorry to bother you ladies, but I wished to speak with you all as a matter of urgency," Flora looked up into the eyes of the man at their door, wondering for a moment if he shouldn't look rather more… grief-stricken. As it was, Lars had the air of someone who had nothing but business on his mind, and he swept past Flora before she could speak a word of invitation or otherwise.

"Mr. Hansen, shouldn't you be with your mother, ah with her body, or something?" Tanya said, before quickly adding, "We are so sorry for your loss."

"Such a lovely woman," Jean added, as Flora took her seat.

"Well, the forensics team are in there now and I can be of little help. Procedures must be followed. I had a couple of things to discuss with you, if you don't mind?"

Assuming it was to do with his mother's last hour, Flora nodded in sympathy, though she caught the look that Tanya shot Jean, no doubt prompted by the man's apparent brashness, "Of course."

"First I wish to extend my apologies, and those of our venue for the unfortunate incident which you were witness to," Lars lowered himself onto a chair at the small dining table near to them, his back straight and his eyes as clear and piercing as ever.

"Well, there is no need, your family have suffered such a tragic bereavem..." Jean began, but was cut off by their visitor.

"My sincere apologies. Obviously, your stay with us will be free of charge, in return for a good review for the hotel which does not mention any of this… unpleasantness."

"Unpleasantness?" Tanya practically spat the word at him and Reggie, sensing her mood, joined in with "Here's the jerk! The fool has arrived!"

"Reginald Parrot!" Flora scolded him, trying to hide her own shock at the man's indifference.

"A review?" Jean asked, her tone as cold as ice and quite out of character.

"Ja, we are just starting out you see and any future guests, or buyers even…"

"I understand the purpose of reviews, Mr. Hansen, but I do wonder why the reputation of the hotel seems to be the first thing on your mind?" Jean continued, and Flora was grateful for her friend's clear-headedness. She herself felt nauseous all over again.

"Well, the other thing," he continued, ignoring the probe completely, "is that the chef is, ah, absent for the evening. So, I will have a light supper delivered here to your room."

"Absent?" Tanya asked, "As in absent under police

custody, because if that's the case, then they can let our friend go…"

"No, I mean, well he has not been present since last night in fact," Lars stood suddenly and made to leave.

"Stupid git!" Reggie shouted after him, and Flora was inclined to agree with the bird for once.

"I just can't believe the barefaced cheek of the man, the audacity to talk about reviews when his mother is barely cold yet," Jean exclaimed when Lars had made a quick exit to the sound of Reggie's abuse chasing him out.

"Absolutely," Flora agreed, "but what's almost stranger is that I saw Hailey rushing out of the kitchen looking rather dishevelled earlier today. Coupled with the fact she seemed to be away from her post more often than not, I assumed she and the chef were having an altercation. I caught him trying to chat her up yesterday in reception and from the sound of it his advances were rather persistent and certainly weren't welcomed."

"Really? Well that doesn't add up then," Jean's brow was pinched and her expression thoughtful, "Perhaps he made a quick disappearance a bit later in the day."

All three woman exchanged knowing glances to confirm they understood her implication. There was much to ponder here, not least poor Betty's predicament and finding justice for Ingrid.

If her son wouldn't do it, then Flora knew she herself would.

TWELVE

It had been an understandably sombre evening, with none of the women having much appetite, and no news on Betty despite all three of them having phoned the police station on different occasions. No one had come to take them to be interviewed again, and when they had phoned down to reception Hailey had abruptly told them that they weren't a priority right now and refused to put one of the officers on the line. This had angered Tanya greatly, and she had been about to go and find Lars Hansen, until Jean reminded her that the man couldn't have been less interested in the case if he'd tried.

Flora had showered and changed into her summer

pyjamas, which were already stuck to her back like glue from the unremitting heat of the day which, as yet, had refused to taper.

She sighed heavily as she put down the book she had been trying and failing to read, "Perhaps if we get an early night, things will seem clearer in the morning?"

"I'm not sure if I'll be able to sleep to be honest," Jean replied, "but we should certainly get some rest."

"One more cup of Earl Grey and we'll settle down for the night," Tanya said, giving Reggie a large grape from their little refrigerator and earning herself the title of "Sexy beast" which he loudly bestowed upon her.

When there was a knock on the door five minutes later, none of the women rushed to answer it. The chances were it was either the police finally come to speak to them, or Lars having thought of another way to safeguard the hotel from any bad publicity. Neither of which they had the strength to face right now. Even Reggie hid his head under his wing in uncharacteristic silence.

"Jean? Flora?" A familiar voice called from the hallway, causing all three women to release a collective, "Oh!" and to rush for the door, though it was Tanya who got there first.

"Harry!" she exclaimed, flinging her arms around the person standing in the corridor, who was still out of sight for Flora, "How did they let you in here?"

"Well, I had insider help," Harry said, coming into the room and nodding behind him.

Sure enough, he was followed by none other than Flora's own man of the moment, "Adam!"

She hurried forwards and threw herself into her fiancé's arms in a rather embarrassing show of affection – not that Flora could have cared less at this point, and seemingly neither could he. Adam wrapped Flora in his embrace and snuggled her against his chest as she tried to make sense of it all.

"But how did Harry get hold of you and how did you get back to Baker's Rise so fast, I…"

"Whoa, slow down a minute love, and I'll explain everything," Adam sent a quick nod to Harry and something unspoken flashed between the two men, but Flora was too relieved to try to interpret the gesture.

"Welcome to the tearoom! So cosy!" Reggie chirped happily from Harry's arm, clearly equally relieved by the upturn of the general atmosphere in the room.

"Silly bird," Tanya declared, though she too sported a

watery smile.

It wasn't that they needed men to rescue them, Flora reassured herself silently as she brewed the tea while Jean updated the newcomers on what they knew of Betty's situation – she was an independent woman, after all – but rather it felt good to have additional support and to know that Betty would feel much better when she could see and speak to her husband.

"So, tell me how you come to be here, I can't tell you how happy I am to see you," Flora said again, when Harry had gone downstairs to try to find one of the detectives.

"Well, ah, there's not much to tell," Adam began, his eyes not quite meeting hers, "a couple of days ago, I felt that I'd done my grieving – not that it's over, or ever will be, but you know what I mean – and my thinking, and I just felt so... lonely, to be honest. I missed Baker's Rise, I missed your cosy coach house and little tearoom. So, I thought I'd come back a few days early and relieve Harry from the bookshop – though he's been doing a grand job, I might add. So have those two new ladies in the tearoom, I think, though Sally was a bit vague on that when I saw her. Anyway, I got back, ah, yesterday actually, and happened to be with Harry today when he got Jean's call. We came straight down."

"Well, I'm thankful for it. Such a tragedy, Adam, the hotel owner Ingrid, the, ah, deceased, was so lovely. It's a shame the same can't be said for her son," Flora noted with sadness that Adam hadn't included her in the list of things he had missed, but hid her disappointment. Nor did she pick him up on the fact that he had clearly had time to visit the vicar's wife but not to call her. *Perhaps he wanted some private bereavement counselling from the vicar,* Flora thought as her brain pulled her in too many different tangents at once.

"Yes, I did have the displeasure of meeting him on my way in. The police officer on the door let us in when I explained and showed my badge, but the Swedish guy – Hansen, is it? – wasted no time in informing me that this suite was the only accommodation available, and that I'd better not be from the press!" Adam continued, oblivious to Flora's inner turmoil.

"Yes, he's a piece of work that's for sure," Flora shook her head sadly, "and I have no idea why this is the only bedroom available. The girl on the desk hinted that this was the only one that had been renovated, but then why would you deck out a whole brand new baking studio before you even have the bedrooms ready? It seems a bit topsy turvy to me."

"Hmm, that it does. It doesn't help with the sleeping arrangements, though. Since you and the ladies have to stay here, I think it's best if Harry and I look for somewhere else to bed down and we can meet back up in the morning," Adam said matter-of-factly and Flora wished he had seemed a little more forlorn about it.

"What? No, really, I mean there's a murderer here and…"

"And when has the little issue of a murderer on the loose ever bothered you?" Adam asked playfully, and Flora couldn't help a wry smile even though she could tell he was trying to detract her from the main point. She had the distinct impression, in fact, that he was keen to get out of there.

"This was meant to be our honeymoon suite," the words were out before Flora could think to stop them.

"Aye love," a shadow crossed Adam's face and he stood abruptly as Harry entered the room and made a beeline for them.

"They're letting me in to see her, but they're keeping her overnight Adam, that can't be a good sign?" Harry's face was white and all of a sudden he looked his age, his sprightly demeanour vanished, though Flora hoped this would only be a temporary change.

"I'll come to the station with you," Adam replied, without missing a beat, "they might let me speak to her."

"Then you'll fill us in tomorrow, first thing?" Flora asked, aware she sounded like a needy child.

"Of course," Harry answered for them both.

"There's a Bible in the drawer in the bedroom, with the details of the local vicarage, so I acted on impulse and called that vicar we met yesterday. Reverend Bloom says she'd be happy to have you two gents stay there for as many nights as you need," Jean said, coming back through from the bedroom, where she and Tanya had gone to give Flora and Adam a moment to catch up.

Flora was eternally grateful for her friend's practical nature and calm in a crisis, hoping even that some of it might rub off on her. Yet a part of her wished that, in this instance, a solution hadn't been so readily come by.

"That's sorted then and we'll take little Tina with us," Harry added, "she'll be needing a walk."

"As soon as we're free to leave here in the morning, we'll meet you at the vicarage," Jean said, a large yawn escaping her lips as she spoke, "my apologies, perhaps I will be able to sleep after all. Especially now I know things are more in hand."

"We're a team!" Reggie screeched as the men left the room, seemingly feeling as bereft as Flora at their quick exit.

"We are," Tanya reassured him, stroking his head feathers.

So why did Flora feel like there was something Adam wasn't telling her?

THIRTEEN

The three women were up and dressed early, anticipating another difficult day ahead of them. A good job too, it turned out to be, as a sharp rap on the door permeated the peace at eight o'clock sharp.

"Get out of it!" Reggie grumbled from his spot beside the window, clearly hoping for more beauty sleep.

Jean answered the door to a short, spectacled girl, wearing a similar receptionist's uniform to Hailey but sporting an agency badge, "Good morning, can I help you?"

The girl, who looked to be no more than seventeen, was wringing her hands together and took a long moment before she replied, "Yes, ah madam I've to tell you that the chef is not here and so breakfast is continuenen... is pastries and stuff and then the policewoman – the scary one – would like a word with you all. Please madam. Thank you." She did a little curtsy and scarpered back down the corridor before Jean could reply.

"I don't think I could eat a full English this morning anyway," Tanya said, as they gathered their bags and sunhats, "a continental breakfast will suit just fine."

Flora agreed, though had no idea how she would keep Reggie away from the plate of fruit that would no doubt form part of the food offering. *Perhaps it would be better to put him in the laundry room, just until the meal and interviews are over*, she thought to herself, cajoling the bird into his carrier with a piece of banana and closing her ears to his – many and varied – protestations.

The laundry room had been a bad idea. Very bad. The worst in fact.

Flora ran back along the corridor to the dining room, bird and carrier in tow, as her mind whirred and her stomach heaved. If she had wondered why Hailey had been replaced at short notice, then she had found her answer – unfortunately the young woman herself could no longer provide any further explanation, though, being as she was currently dead, and stuffed into a large wicker hamper.

"Here, take Reggie," Flora unceremoniously thrust the carrier into Tanya's hands before rushing back out of the dining room in search of Detective Matlock.

"There is no need to run around like a headless chicken, Mrs. Miller, one of my officers will come for you when we have finished interviewing the local ladies. Mrs. Glendinning is being very helpful indeed."

"It sounds it," Flora responded with sarcasm, as the piping tones of Violet Glendinning could be heard from the nearby room, accusing her interviewer of 'having no right questioning her.'

"…I am the head of the parish council and wife to the local bank manager, you know!"

"No, I meant regarding the fact she has been furnishing us with details of an argument which your Mrs. Bentley had with the deceased at the start of yesterday's baking class," Matlock clarified, "clearly Mrs. Glendinning simply has interview fatigue – it can be very tiring answering endless questions… when you're innocent." The last was said in a pointed fashion, but Flora's mind was fixated on the detective's first claim.

"Betty? Arguing?" Flora parroted the words back to her, no doubt confirming the woman's suspicion that she was dim-witted, "No! She just likes to rule the roost a bit where baking is concerned, likes to be the one who knows the most, there was no argument…argh! Why am I even talking about this? I came to find you for a specific reason, Detective."

"Yes, I understand that you have a pet parrot who can't be cooped up in the room, blah blah blah, Mr. Hansen has also tried to persuade me to let you all leave as soon as possible."

"What? No! There's a body!"

"Yes, dear, I know, I've been investigating the death for almost twenty-four hours now," she spoke slowly, enunciating each word as if to a child.

"A new body!" Flora was shrieking now, causing the new receptionist who was hovering behind the desk, looking at a loss as to what she should be doing, to burst into tears and run towards the main entrance. To be fair, Flora felt like joining her.

For the first time that morning, Detective Matlock gave Flora her full attention, "A new body? And you have seen it?" She did nothing to try to hide the suspicion in her voice, and Flora felt like her legs might go out from under her.

"Flora? Is everything okay?" Thankfully, Jean came to the rescue.

"There is apparently a new body," the detective said dryly, "tell me, did your friend take any sleeping tablets?"

Before Jean could credit the question with an answer, Flora straightened her back, looked Matlock in the eye and said clearly, "The body of the receptionist, Hailey, is in the laundry room. It appears she has been strangled by the oversized shirt she was wearing yesterday."

If the place had been buzzing with activity before, it was now a positive hive of commotion. Flora, Tanya and Jean sat quietly around their table in the bay window of the dining room, taking turns to offer Reggie pieces of fruit to keep him quiet. The bird himself seemed to think Christmas had come early, and strutted up and down the tablecloth – the same one from yesterday, judging by the coffee pot stains – as if he had finally figured out the secret to life, the universe and everything. Flora no longer cared that giving him freedom to roam probably wasn't hygienic and certainly wasn't appropriate, she merely stared into the bottom of her empty coffee cup and willed Adam to respond quickly to the text she had sent.

Her silent pleas were evidently not heard, however, as two minutes later she was summoned into the baking studio – one end of which had been turned into a makeshift office with a desk and chairs, there being no sign of Mrs. Glendinning in there now – to face Detective Matlock and her sidekick, who was introduced as Detective Cluero. The fact that this second investigator's name sounded rather like the French fictional character Inspector Clouseau and also very similar to the game Cluedo struck Flora as funny and she let out a small snort. Mortified, she couldn't help the even louder giggle which followed it, and Flora wondered if she might actually be going mad this time.

"Are you quite well, Madam?" Cluero asked, though in a kinder voice than Flora would have credited him for.

"Yes, well, all things considered," Flora shrugged her

shoulders, hoping that the simple action could convey the horror of seeing two dead bodies in as many days.

"If you don't mind, we will go back over the events of yesterday morning, and then we will need to ask you some questions as to your whereabouts yesterday evening and during the night," he spoke softly and clearly, his Welsh lilt a balm to his colleague's constant, harsh glare.

"My whereabouts? I was in the bedroom where you put me. With my friends. But ah, okay, fire away," Flora took a deep breath and let it out slowly.

She was becoming an old hand at this interview thing now.

FOURTEEN

"I've said I'm sorry. Apologised three times in fact. The truth is that we were at the station getting Betty," Adam was clearly losing his patience now, and Flora did feel rather guilty for it.

She had done nothing but question him and his delay in getting back to the hotel since the moment he arrived with Harry and Betty, which had been at the end of her ninety minute interview with the police. To say she was frazzled was an understatement, though Flora knew that was no excuse for her behaviour.

"I know, and I'm the one who should be sorry," Flora dabbed her sweaty forehead with the back of her hand,

"I hope Betty's okay... and the others. Goodness knows how long they'll be downstairs with the detectives."

"Aye well, love, Betty will feel better once she's had her long soak in the bath, and when Harry gets back with those teacakes and the parkin he promised her from the bakery."

"It's so awful, Adam, did she say anything to you both in car?"

"Only that she was tired but that she can't sleep because every time there's a moment of quiet she hears the deceased woman's last words."

"What were they?" Flora asked, wondering briefly if the question wasn't too macabre.

"Betty says that Ingrid said 'help me' in her own language and Betty tried to stem the bleeding, but there were too many wounds in the victim's chest and no hope of staunching the flow. I know Betty feels guilty about that, but there really wasn't anything she could do. The attack must've been frenzied. Definitely an amateur I would say."

"Do you think it was someone who knew Ingrid?" Flora asked, a chill running down her spine.

"Likely so, love," Adam put his arm around her shoulders and Flora felt only slightly warmer, "try not to think on it."

"But poor Hailey as well, could it be the same person who... got them both?"

"Well, they aren't doing a good job of covering their tracks if it was. Two haphazard killings, on the same day and in the same location, that can't have been planned out surely? I'd be very surprised if there aren't any fingerprints found at either of the scenes."

"But won't the people who work here have their fingerprints all over anyway?"

"Hmm," was all Adam replied, and Flora fell silent.

Flora had been given a reprieve and was allowed to walk Reggie around the front gardens of the hotel. Having returned from being interviewed, Jean was talking with Betty and Harry in the suite, Tanya had gone for a lie down, and so it was just her and Adam. Except the man himself had disappeared again, apparently needing to 'get some air.'

"Wasn't that exactly what we were about to do?" Flora asked Reggie, not that she expected an answer, as the bird was already hovering well above her head as they entered the hotel foyer.

"Adventure awaits!" He squawked, completely oblivious to how far that now was from the truth of their situation.

"Pipe down! Please shut your beak," Flora snapped back, regretting her tone instantly as Reggie took off without a backward glance the moment they were out of the main doors.

I'm even talking in parrot lingo now, Flora noted, to her own annoyance, as she sat on one of the outdoor benches that flanked the entryway. She knew Reggie wouldn't go far from his seed source – if ever a bird was ruled by his tummy it was that one – and so she sat down for a much needed breather. A small, coastal breeze hit the side of her face, and Flora turned in that direction so that she would feel its cooling effect fully. In doing so, however, she came upon a conversation that had hitherto been too quiet for her to pick up on.

"Yes, the whole block of them has gone. The team have logged them as present in their sweep of the kitchens yesterday, minus the ten inch knife that was already found at the first crime scene of course, which means he must've come back last night for them… yes, looks like our man and you know how chefs are about their knives, looks like it'll work out to our benefit... just waiting for the lab report on the second scene. He could be counties away by now though, we need to act fast..."

The voice became louder, but too quickly for Flora to move, so it was a rather angry detective who quickly ended her call and stood, hands on hips in front of Flora now.

"Mrs. Miller, how long have you been sitting here?"

"Oh, just a moment, my parrot is stretching his wings..."

With perfect timing as per usual, Reggie chose that moment to divebomb the policewoman, sweeping just above her scraped-back and greased down hair, and shrieking "You old trout!" as he took off once again for the skies.

Detective Matlock jumped backwards, her hand going to her side no doubt for a weapon, but by then Reggie was up in the sky again, swooping and weaving as if nothing had happened.

"What the hel..?" Matlock shouted.

"Believe me, that could've been much worse," again, Flora found the sudden and inappropriate urge to giggle, but at least managed to contain it this time, "yes, just getting some fresh air and exercise, the heat seems to be tempered by a breeze at last." Flora smiled up innocently, hoping that she gave the impression she knew nothing, had heard nothing, and wished to know nothing.

Whether she was convinced or not, Matlock huffed out a sigh, gave Flora one final glare and stomped past into the hotel, a small voice shouting "Good riddance" to her from above.

Flora was inclined to agree.

Armed with this new information, Flora stood with the intention of rushing back upstairs as soon as Reggie could be coaxed from his flight. In a rather schoolgirl error, though, she had not brought any fruit out with her with which to bribe the greedy bird. Luckily, however, and in the first well-timed moment of Flora's day, the gardener appeared from the opposite side of the building, a bag of fish and chips from the pier fishery in hand. Whether Reggie had perfect vision, an astounding sense of smell, or just a sixth stomach sense, Flora wasn't sure, but there he was, back on her shoulder the moment food appeared.

Flora recognised the man as the one she had seen talking with Lars outside, and wondered if he might know anything else about the case. *Well, it's important that Betty is completely cleared*, Flora told herself, as if trying to justify putting her nose where it wasn't required.

"You're my honey!" Reggie said, bobbing up and down excitedly and angling towards the stranger.

"Well, aren't you a strange little chap," the man reminded Flora so much of her late friend Billy, that she had to swallow down a sudden lump in her throat when she heard him speak. Up close, he was much younger than her former gardener – by a good couple of decades at least – but he had the same unassuming posture and gentle demeanour that made Flora feel immediately at ease.

"Yes, he certainly is," Flora smiled as Reggie was offered a piece of fish without the batter.

Delighted, the parrot gulped down the treasured treat and hopped onto the man's arm, "You sexy beast!" he squawked, though Flora wasn't sure if he was talking to the human or his fish platter.

"Reginald Parrot!" Flora scolded, despite knowing her feathered friend would take no heed whatsoever.

"Ah, he's alright, I was finished anyway. I have to be quick, just come to clear out my tools and such," the man said, laying the wrapper out on the bench for Reggie to pick at his leftovers.

"Heavens above! Praise be!" Reggie shrieked at the feast laid out before him. Flora had no idea where he'd heard that phrase, but it seemed strangely apt and she couldn't help smiling again.

"Thank you for that," she said, "but it's a shame you're leaving. Is it because of the murders?" *Subtle Flora, very subtle.*

"No lass, gave me my marching orders yesterday he did. I haven't been paid since the first week they took over, though, so I suppose I've lost nothing. It's just I've enjoyed working here the past few years."

"Oh, I'm sorry. I hope you get the money you're owed," Flora's brain was already whirring.

"I doubt that, but thank you lass," the man tipped his cap at her, patted Reggie on the head – not that the parrot noticed, so busy was he scoffing – and continued round the corner.

"Well, that's worth mentioning..." Flora mused aloud as she scooped up the green glutton, the greasy wrapper still in the firm grasp of his little talons, and carried the whole fishy, feathery package upstairs.

FIFTEEN

"What is that smell?" Tanya asked loudly as she emerged from the bedroom after her nap.

"Ah, that would be Reggie," Flora admitted sheepishly, "he was given some fish and chip bits and although I've managed to throw the wrapper away – and have the scratches to prove it, silly bird – the smell does seem to have lingered on his feathers."

"Lingered? He smells like he's been bathing in the sea," Tanya scrunched her nose distastefully, "there's nothing for it, you need a shower little bird."

Not really understanding the words, but seeing the woman advancing on him with intent, Reggie took off from his perch on the back of Flora's chair and up to the curtain pole where he couldn't be so easily reached.

"I can be patient," Tanya said, sending a wink in his direction, before slumping down in the chair next to Flora.

"Where are the others?" Flora asked.

"Well, I haven't seen Adam since he left before you, but I heard Jean say they were going to stretch their legs about ten minutes ago," Tanya replied, "I'll put the kettle on."

"I could definitely do with a cuppa," Flora rubbed her feet and ankles which had swollen in the heat and was, to her embarrassment, still doing so when the door to the suite opened and Adam entered with the local vicar.

"Reverend Daisy," Flora said, whilst trying and failing to shove her feet back into her sandals, "it's lovely to see you again, we were just going to have a cup of tea."

"Sounds perfect," Daisy leant her multicoloured cane against the table and then lowered herself slowly onto the chair. Catching Flora watching her, she said, "Some days are better than others."

"I'm sorry, I didn't mean to stare."

"Not at all, I'd rather it wasn't the elephant in the room," Daisy smiled brightly, "since you couldn't make it up to the vicarage this morning I thought I'd come to see how you're all doing and to pass my condolences to the family. Such an awful business."

"I'm surprised they let you in," Tanya said, handing her a mug of tea and placing some sugar sachets and plastic milk pots on the table.

"Ah well, perks of the job, I guess, if you could use that term in cases like this," Daisy tapped her dog collar, "though I must admit to preferring weddings and christenings." She shot a happy look in Adam's direction, where he stood by the window, but Flora was too busy watching her parrot who had taken a sudden interest in the vicar's walking stick. Finding the courage to come down from the safety of the curtain rail while Tanya was otherwise distracted, the bird was waddling up and down in front of the bright mobility aid, bobbing his head and chattering away as if the stick was a creature which would respond to his charms.

Flora found herself laughing at his antics, as did Daisy, while even Tanya couldn't help a chuckle. Their mirth was short-lived, however, when a sharp rap on the door brought an immediate silence to the room.

"I'll get it," Adam said, already halfway to the door.

The sudden churning in Flora's stomach told her this wasn't another social visit, and she was right.

And so Flora found herself in a police car on her way to the local station. She couldn't tell which were throbbing the worst – her feet or her head, but either way it was making her miserable. That and the fact that she hadn't been allowed anyone to come with her. Betty, Harry and Jean had arrived back at the hotel room just as the uniformed officer was explaining that Flora needed to accompany her and her colleague in order to give a full statement for finding the body of the receptionist.

The trauma of seeing her friend being led away, though not in cuffs and only temporarily, seemed to affect Betty badly and she broke down in tears on Harry's shoulder. This then caused Flora's own anxiety to bubble over and soon there were a lot of emotions on display, and yet the young woman who had come to fetch Flora appeared indifferent to it all.

"Get it over and done with, love," Adam had said, kissing his fiancée on the forehead, "sooner this is all resolved, sooner we can get out of here. The moment you're done let me know and I'll come to collect you."

"You're welcome up at the vicarage any time," Daisy had added in her soothing voice, and then Flora had had to leave her friends behind.

The journey was thankfully brief, and before Flora had really registered it she was being asked to take a seat in the tiny reception area. The station was much smaller than she had anticipated and Flora deduced that there wasn't normally much crime in the area. *The detectives have probably had to come across from a bigger town such as Whitby or Scarborough,* she thought, eager to keep her mind off the fact that she was going to have to relive recent events once again during her interview.

As if her wish was granted, a distraction appeared then in the form of Detective Matlock, who led in a small, irate man in handcuffs – whom Flora immediately recognised as none other than Pierre, the chef from the hotel.

Totally ignoring Flora, she marched up to the desk with a satisfied expression, like the cat that got the cream, and announced, "We have him!"

The desk sergeant, who seemed completely nonplussed, took his time walking over to the Perspex screen, and simply buzzed them through to the secure area, though not before Flora tuned into the fact that the chef was shouting and railing against his arrest.

"I tells you again, I did not kill ze boss! I was not even in ze building yesterday mornings. My car was broken in…"

"Now, Mr. Faucher, there will be plenty of time for you to state your case in the interview room. Remember your right to remain silent. You can call a lawyer to act on your behalf…" the calming tones of Detective Cluero followed the detainee into the area now, so that Flora had to turn her knees sideways to accommodate all three next to her in the small space.

"Ah, Mrs. Miller, apologies for the delay, I will be with you shortly," the pleasant detective smiled, putting Flora slightly more at ease, as the chef was led into the main body of the station and the door clanged shut after Cluero.

Well, that's interesting, Flora thought to herself, unable to stop her mind from speculating, *if they've arrested him for both murders, but he denies the first… will Betty still be implicated? And if the chef wasn't in the kitchen, then who was Hailey in there with on the morning of Ingrid's death?*

The wall clock ticked the minutes by, the sun went

down outside the single, high window, and still Flora waited. Thankfully, her anxiety had finally settled, helped by a cup of sweet tea which the kind desk sergeant had offered, and she had resigned herself to the now-familiar process.

One thing remained at the forefront of her mind – to find the justice for Ingrid that her son clearly had no interest in seeking, and to do so quickly, so that Betty wouldn't be brought back in here. Simple.

It might just require a little bit of investigation…

SIXTEEN

"So we are free to leave?" Betty repeated the detective's words back to her for the second time, as if she couldn't quite believe their meaning. She clutched little Tina to her chest like a shield, stroking the dog's head absentmindedly.

"As I said, we have the suspect for both murders in custody and you are free to come and go as you please. I have all of your statements," the detective didn't even try to keep the exasperation from her voice.

"Come on love, let's get your things together," Harry led Betty away from the door to the suite, as Matlock turned and left without saying a further word to Flora, who had been standing at the entrance to their room with her friend.

It was barely nine in the morning, though Flora had not slept. It had been only a few hours since she had finished at the station and Adam had come to get her. Harry had slept next to Betty on the double bed while the other two women took the makeshift beds. Not wanting to disturb them, Adam had taken a detour before going back to the hotel and had parked up by the seafront so that he and Flora could watch the sunrise over the North Sea together.

To be honest, Flora was still reeling from what her fiancé had shared in that special moment and, coupled with the lack of sleep, she was feeling quite lightheaded.

Reggie had no such issues. He was full of the joys of life, having sniffed out the packaging from yesterday's takeaway and slept cocooned in it in the wastepaper bin. Unfortunately, this had not helped his smell and he now positively reeked.

"Ha! Now I have you!" Tanya pounced on the bird, cupping her hands to scoop him up and carry him to the sink in the bathroom for a much needed wash.

"I can help you…" Flora offered, but there was no

conviction in her voice.

"No, no, you get packed and then we can all get out of here," Tanya smiled and Flora was grateful for her friend's help. Certainly, none of them wanted to share a hot car with a fishy bird!

"Actually," Adam began, holding out his hand to Flora, "would you all mind if we stayed for a few more days?"

Everyone stood still for a moment, staring at the man as if he had just developed a second head.

"You mean, stay here, in Lillymouth, and not head straight home to Baker's Rise?" Jean clarified, her eyes wide with surprise.

"Well yes, I mean, not in this hotel, obviously," Adam hastened to add, "I've phoned the Crow's Nest Inn up the road and they have free rooms. I'll be taking care of the bill, it's just that... well... I've been planning a surprise for Flora. Not for long, mind you, just for the past few days, and it relies on us all being here on Friday."

"And what would that be?" Tanya asked, poised in the doorway to the bathroom, and suffering the verbal abuse of the bird in her hold.

"You bad bird! My Flora!" he shrieked plaintively, clearly hoping to be rescued from the horror of his watery fate.

They all ignored him, eyes fixed on the pair in the middle of the room.

"Well, the reason I was already back in Baker's Rise, and had actually planned on coming down here with Harry later in the week, was that I wanted you all here to witness us getting married," Adam's face was beet red and there were droplets of sweat dripping down his forehead. Nevertheless, to Flora he had never looked more handsome, "I realised on my wanderings that our time down here is too short. You have to seize life and love with both hands while you can. I spoke with Reverend Daisy earlier at the vicarage and she is very happy to perform the service, even helped me sort the licence."

"He's even thought to bring me something to wear!" Flora gushed, overcome with happiness and wiping away the stray leakage from her eyes, "Went shopping in Morpeth with Sally and everything!"

"Aw, of course we'll stay lass," Betty answered for them all, "and has there been a small wedding breakfast or reception organised? An afternoon tea or suchlike?" Her old eyes twinkled hopefully.

"Actually, Reverend Daisy has very kindly offered you ladies the use of the vicarage kitchen to rustle something up, if you wouldn't mind?" Adam replied, winking at the older woman and knowing fine well the response he would receive.

"Mind?" Betty was back to being the animated version that Flora knew and loved, "Mind? It would be our pleasure! You don't need any shop bought bakes when you have two experienced ladies of the W.I. – Jean and I have a combined knowledge of over a hundred years, did you know that..?" And she was off, in her element, and Flora couldn't have been happier. She accepted Adam's sweet kiss and felt the butterflies of their upcoming nuptials down to her toes.

She would keep the other bit of news that Adam had shared in the car close to her chest for the time being, in case he changed his mind.

The Crow's Nest Inn was full of the quaint English charm that the villagers were used to. The bedrooms were a celebration of chintz and lace, the main bar area was adorned with black and white photos of the area's centuries-old smuggling history, and the proprietor had a beer belly to match his over-inflated ego. They felt like they had come home!

Reggie had recovered from his apparent ordeal and now smelt like lemon verbena. Tanya, however, was still drying off in the sun, her once-pristine curls looking decidedly lacklustre – apparently wings and water can make quite a splash effect! Flora wished she had recorded the conversation that could be heard from the bathroom, could have probably been heard throughout the whole hotel, in fact, with Tanya and Reggie sparring with words throughout the whole bathing session.

The local residents and tourists enjoying a drink in the inn's beer garden were quite enamoured with the cheeky chap, though, encouraging him to land on the wooden picnic tables and feeding him crumbs of their pub grub. Of course, Reggie was in his element, strutting up and down the tables and even serenading his audience with an impromptu rendition of Elvis' 'Love Me Tender'. Phones and cameras were held up to capture the moment, and Flora had the sinking feeling that her extroverted pet was about to become a social media star.

Nevertheless, relaxed for the first time in days and with a frisson of excitement running through her, Flora sipped on her white wine spritzer and enjoyed the other spectacle of the inn's owner trying to flirt with Tanya. Her friend was having none of it, of course, and her scathing replies were keeping them all amused.

"Sup up love and we'll take a walk down to the vicarage, shall we? Daisy said we could call down and chat over the details of the wedding service, and that there's a florist in town where you could order some flowers if you like," he lifted her hand which had been entwined in his for most of the morning and kissed Flora's palm gently.

"Sounds perfect... Adam, can I ask you a question?" Flora lowered her voice so that only he could hear, leaning close to whisper into her fiancé's ear.

"Anything love, do you want to go somewhere more private?"

"No, ah, no it's not that kind of question," Flora felt herself blush, even though her mind had gone to certain places without any prompting whatsoever, "it's a police type question actually."

"We're on holiday, Flora, and about to get married... but I did say ask me anything, so fire away, I guess."

"Thank you, well, when you've finished a case, does it ever niggle at you? Like your mind isn't ready to let it go? As if the outcome doesn't seem to quite fit for some reason?"

"Sometimes, lass, yes. And I have to admit I normally follow that gut feeling – if the case doesn't feel properly resolved, I keep going until it does. It's my responsibility to make sure that the right people are put behind bars. I'm guessing you have that feeling now?"

"Well, of course, my overriding emotion right at this minute is happiness," Flora was quick to reassure him, "but underneath, there's this awful feeling that I can't shake."

"Do you know what exact facts might be prompting that feeling?"

Flora was grateful that he was taking her seriously – not that Adam had ever not treated her as an equal, but she had been considered a hysterical woman so much in the last few days, that Flora had been starting to get used to it.

"Well, Lars gives me bad vibes, has done since we first got here. He didn't treat Ingrid with respect…" Flora explained the conversation she and Tanya had overheard in the park, "… and there's the question of the finances. I think he might be doing some dubious accounting, or at least someone somewhere is. Pierre was adamant at the station that he hadn't killed Ingrid, so could it have been her son?"

"Well, I have to say he gave me an off feeling too, so I did have a quiet word with Cluero not long after I arrived – nice guy, met the man on a few training courses in the past – thinking surely Hansen must be their main suspect and not some septuagenarian with an overly-zealous passion for baking, but apparently the man has an alibi. He and the receptionist were working together on a new marketing brochure. They were each other's alibi in fact."

"Hmm," that wasn't really what Flora wanted to hear, but she couldn't offer an alternative suggestion, "I guess I just dislike the man and was angry at the way he treated his mother. It all just seems too… cut and dried."

"I hear you, love, but if the detectives in the case share your concerns, you can be sure they'll look into it. Unfortunately, there are plenty of narcissistic and unkind people in the world who don't do anything worth locking them up for. I do love how you care so deeply though."

"Ha, some might call it nosiness!"

"Yes, well, not me," he leant over and kissed her quickly, "right, drink up, we've got a wedding to plan!"

SEVENTEEN

It took several minutes of cajoling and eventual bribery with a scampi bite before Reggie was amenable to accompanying Flora and Adam to the centre of the town. They set off on foot, with the little bird travelling happily on Adam's shoulder, bobbing up and down excitedly and chirping to himself none stop, clearly pleased with his recent efforts at demonstrating his showmanship.

"Good bird! Funny lad!" He repeated over and over, "Do it again!" Flora would rather he didn't do it again, to be honest, but she appreciated his good humour, as it matched her own.

There were more white clouds overhead now and the

breeze had picked up, making the stroll actually quite pleasant. They paused on the ancient stone bridge over the Lillywater river and took in the view from both sides – on the one, the river opened up through the small harbour and into the sea, channelled through the two piers. At the end of each of these, a lighthouse stood tall and proud, seagulls swirling overhead making it a picture-perfect scene.

"Would you like to take a walk down the pier, love, after we've seen the vicar?" Adam asked.

"Perhaps," Flora replied, linking arms with her fiancé and moving on again. To be honest, the idea sounded lovely, from every perspective but that of her poor feet, so Flora didn't want to commit herself, best to see how she felt later, "the park's just up ahead though, we could always take a small detour through there on our way to the vicarage, if you like?"

"Sounds perfect. To be honest, just being with you again is perfect," Adam smiled widely, with Flora mirroring his expression.

They walked to the bandstand – thankfully, there were no arguments going on there today – and then cut back onto the cobbles of Front Street, pausing outside of Bea's Book Nook, where Flora described the visit they had made there shortly after the women's arrival in the town.

"Would you like some new baking books? Or maybe to browse the travel section to get some ideas for our proper honeymoon?" Adam asked.

"Honeymoon? Oh! I hadn't thought, I mean… yes! That sounds lovely," Flora led them into the cool, darker interior of the shop, immediately feeling the same sense of calm and welcome she had felt a few days ago. A teenager with bright green hair stood behind the counter now, blowing a bubble with her gum and looking thoroughly bored with life.

"Welcome to the tearoom!" Reggie squawked happily, clearly remembering the place.

"Why don't you finish off for the day, Katie," Bea's voice came from down the far end of the shop, in the tea and coffee corner, "it's been so quiet, you might as well."

"K, thanks," the girl muttered, reaching under the bench to pull out a tiny backpack and then squeezing past them both without a word of welcome or goodbye.

"Flora!" Bea exclaimed as she came into view walking towards the front of the shop, little Daisy Mae strapped to her front again, "Hello, come in, have you both had lunch yet?"

"Oh, I hadn't even thought about that," Flora replied, though her stomach answered for her with a loud rumble at that very moment.

"We'd love some," Adam answered, grinning, "Adam Bramble, lovely to meet you."

"Oh yes, sorry, Bea meet my fiancé, very soon to be my husband," it felt so good saying those words.

"Abigail Freeman, pleased to meet you," she led them past the beautiful rows of wooden bookshelves and high, panelled alcoves, to the back of the room where they had the choice of every table as all were free, "ah, we're having a quiet day today." The look of sadness and worry in the young woman's eyes was unmistakable, though transformed quickly as she handed them a menu.

"Just a scone would do," Flora said kindly.

"Actually, I've expanded the menu with sandwiches from a new deli that's opened up just up the road, and since I've no customers they all need eating…" Bea said, her hopeful expression one that Flora could certainly sympathise with from her own experience of running a tearoom. It seemed you either overbought or underbaked, guessing how many customers you would have on any given week, in any particular season was always an ongoing task. Then when you tried something new to attract more trade, there was always the chance no one would like it…

"Well, that sounds perfect," Adam answered for them both.

"Yes," Flora added, "and will you and your gorgeous daughter join us?"

"Oh, that would be lovely," Bea's smile reached her pretty eyes this time, and her shoulders relaxed slightly, "my husband is working over near Whitby at the moment, so it means long days."

"I can relate to that, what is it that he does?" Adam asked.

"House renovations, mainly, he's a carpenter so he's often asked to work on wooden rails and banisters, kitchens, wardrobes… anything the owners want in keeping with the original timeframe of the property really. Or else, it's for people who want something completely bespoke. He made these units here where I can store everything for this tea nook," Bea swept her hand past the wall behind them proudly, where some beautiful wooden cabinetry stood, in complete keeping with the rest of the place.

"Wow, those are beautiful," Flora said, her mind whirring with ideas for her own properties.

"They are that, why don't you direct me to the coffee machine and the food, and sit and chat with Flora while I get us sorted?" Adam asked.

"Actually, that would be perfect," Bea let out a small sigh of relief, "it's just a basic percolator at the moment right there behind the first long door on the left, the old coffee machine finally gave up the ghost yesterday, and the sandwiches are in the small fridge down on your right, just take your pick."

"So you mean it's not the first murder here this summer?" Flora asked, taking a sip from her third cup of coffee. She was going to be buzzing all afternoon now, she knew, if not from wedding excitement then certainly from the caffeine.

"No, unfortunately not," Bea continued, as her two guests listened intently, Adam rocking little Daisy Mae in his arms – a sight which touched Flora more than she cared to admit to herself, "though the culprit in the other case is thankfully behind bars now – down to my Daisy of all people! I never saw her as an amateur sleuth, but I think she had no choice but to get involved because the crime happened on church property."

Flora was intrigued, but could tell that Adam was itching to get on the move again as he had stopped adding to the conversation a few minutes ago. She knew he didn't enjoy talking 'shop' when he was away from work. Besides, Reggie too had taken to doing long sweeps of the room, the offering of crumbs at the table having dried up. Before Flora could reply, however, the bell above the door at the other end of the shop tinkled signalling a new customer and it gave them a good excuse to be getting on their way. They expressed their gratitude, insisted on paying, promised to call back tomorrow to have a closer look at the books, and were all but ready to leave when the bell rang again, and Flora found herself face to face with none other than Violet Glendinning.

Adam had never met the woman, so either he recognised her from Flora's description of the events of the day of Ingrid's murder, or he simply noticed how his fiancée was suddenly frozen in tense anger. Either way, he put his arm around Flora's shoulders and whispered, "Let's head on to the florist, Bea says he's just a few doors up."

Flora had no intention of letting this moment pass in silence, however, not with the way the woman had spoken to Ingrid and then deliberately implicated Betty. She shook off Adam's arm, squared her shoulders and…

"You silly old trout! Bad bird!" Reggie spoke for her from his spot next to the antique cash register which Bea kept for show on the main counter.

"Well, you mangy little…"

"Shut yer face! Pipe down you wee maggot!" The parrot was in full flow now, and Flora for once did nothing to stop him. Bea made a muffled cough from behind her hands, which sounded remarkably like a snort of laughter, and Adam simply stood with an amused smile on his face.

"Am I to be insulted?" Violet asked, indignance written across her features.

"Well, since you were so keen to insult Ingrid Hansen, I think you should be able to take as good as you give," Flora spoke up, though her words were almost lost in the noise coming from her pet, who was still continuing his tirade, running through his repertoire of offensive phrases.

"...The fool has arrived! Stupid jerk! Good riddance!" He finally finished, just as it looked like steam might explode from Violet's ears.

Her eyes mere slits and her jaw clenched, the woman turned on her heel and stormed out of the bookshop, slamming the door behind her.

"I'm sorry, I think we may have lost you a customer," Flora said, truly apologetic as she had not intended to harm Bea's business.

"Please don't be, she never buys more than a cup of tea anyway, and even then insists on 'residents' rates' whatever that might be, only ever giving me a single pound coin for my trouble, while telling me how much nicer the place was when my aunt owned it. No, customers like that I can do without," Bea said, shrugging her shoulders and bouncing the increasingly fussy baby up and down.

"We'll leave you to settle her for her nap, thanks again," Flora said, giving Bea a quick hug and then following Adam and Reggie out.

"That Glendinning woman is a piece of work," Flora

said once they were outside, surprising herself slightly with the venom in her own voice.

"People are still people wherever you go, be it little villages or big cities," Adam said sagely as they turned onto the shopping street of Cobble Wynd.

"Aren't they just," Flora agreed, "aren't they just."

EIGHTEEN

The florist was not what Flora had expected, not at all in fact. The man was tall, thin and dressed rather like an undertaker in a straight morning coat over the longest, narrowest pinstripe trousers Flora her ever seen, strongly resembling drainpipes and coupled with a fitted shirt, waistcoat and pocket watch. Her immediate thought was that the man would not be out of place in a horror show, in fact. His booming voice set her head immediately thumping behind her temple, as he announced loudly on their arrival that, "Pets were not permitted!"

"Oh, he won't touch the flowers," Flora said quickly,

hoping that was the truth.

"Tis not... hachew! Hachew!... my stock I fear for, Madam, tis my... hachew! Allergies!"

"Oh," Flora's head began whirring as she tried to focus on the problem at hand. Even the man's sneezes were so loud that they shook the glass vases in the window display.

"Let me take him out while you choose, love. You get whatever you fancy, and add matching buttonholes for me and Harry, would you?" Adam said as he scooped Reggie up quickly from her shoulder before the bird could get wind of the ambush and fly out of reach. Mission accomplished, the pair disappeared back out of the door, leaving Flora with the least floral person she had ever met.

Let's make this quick and simple, Flora told herself, not liking the way the man was eying her up.

"Gerald Bunch," he extended long, bony fingers towards her, which Flora reluctantly shook, making a point of touching as little of the man's cold, pale skin as possible, "so, what's the occasion?"

"Ah, a wedding, my wedding, Friday in fact."

"This week?" Bunch pulled a face of acute displeasure,

"You have left things very late. I like time to plan my creations and I don't have another delivery before then, so we'll have to work with what I've got in stock."

"That's fine, I'm just looking for something simple and classy."

"Madam, everything I make is classy, I'm an artiste!" It was the second time that week Flora had heard someone refer to themselves as such, and it made even less impression on her this time.

"Of course, well ah…" Flora tried to quickly scan the range of vases and pre-assembled bouquets, all the while feeling his eyes on her.

"This Friday, you say? That wouldn't be here with our lovely vicar would it?" The man asked, leaning down and forwards until his pale, thin nose and scraggly-haired chin were level with her own face.

Distracted by the largest, hooded eyes she had ever seen, making him look distinctly like a bird of prey, Flora didn't answer immediately, so the man continued, "Daisy Bloom, what a woman! I'm working on persuading her to make a bunch of blooms with me, if you get my drift," he winked conspiratorially, whilst simultaneously licking his thin, dry lips, making Flora feel queasy. She immediately took two steps back, feeling her legs pressing up against the shelf on which some of the flowers were standing in pots.

"You get it? Gerald Bunch and Daisy Bloom, meant to be!" His loud guffaw rattled the room, and Flora wondered when the man would ever shut up.

"Daisies, yes some of those large-flowered, long-stemmed ones in the window, and lisianthus or purple stocks if you have them, ah, just use your, ah, creative genius to make a small posy please. My fiancé will definitely be the one collecting them and he'll call in the day before the service," Flora flung the door open and practically jumped outside, desperate for some fresh air and to get out of this man's lair.

"All sorted, love?" Adam looked startled at the speed at which his fiancée had accomplished the task.

"Let's just get to the vicarage," Flora walked off ahead, her head pounding and the niggling feeling in her stomach back in full force, though what had triggered it she wasn't sure.

The short walk to the parish Church of St. John the Baptist was a pleasant one, with all three happy to walk in comfortable silence, occupied with their own thoughts. Flora herself couldn't get that strange florist out of her mind, and was glad when they reached the church and Daisy's welcoming smile.

"Come in, come in," she stood under the arch of the old, wooden entrance and gestured with her walking stick for them to follow her inside, "Yes, yes, Reggie too. I just thought we could meet here at the church first and have a quick run though. I mean, you don't need a rehearsal with it being such an intimate service, but I thought you'd like to see where you'll be standing and all that, and then we can go across to the vicarage for some tea and cake."

"That sounds perfect, thank you so much Vicar."

"It is absolutely my pleasure. Are you okay, Flora? You look quite pale. Just wedding nerves?"

"Oh, well yes, and… actually we just met your very strange florist."

"Ah, say no more. Yes, I had that same yucky feeling the first time I met the man too. Not least because he made some, ah, rather lurid suggestions."

"I think I know exactly what you're referring to, as he said the same to me," Flora replied. Seeing Adam's eyebrow fly into his hairline, she quickly added, "Oh, not about me though, about you Daisy actually."

"Eugh, please don't tell me he gave you the whole 'bunches of blooms' speech? It makes me queasy every Sunday when he repeats it like clockwork."

"Well, ah, unfortunately yes."

"I'll have to have another word with him…" Daisy tutted to herself and visibly shuddered, "anyway, let's focus on much more pleasant events, shall we?"

The vicar led them up the main aisle, and Flora breathed in the peace and serenity of the place. The smell of furniture polish, mixed with the strong scent of lilies from the floral arrangements at the front of the chapel, created a familiar and relaxing aroma that Flora was used to from her own place of worship in Baker's Rise.

"Such a beautiful church," Flora whispered, thankful that even Reggie had remained silent and calm, snuggled into her neck.

"Yes, it really is. I grew up here, so it was very familiar to me when I came back."

"How long have you been back in the area?" Adam asked politely.

"Oh, just a couple of months. It's been… eventful, to say the least. And busy. Very busy, as I'm without a curate to help me at the moment."

"Is there a shortage of them within the Church of England?" Flora asked.

"Apparently so. There was a curate here, but ah, they left on a plane to Majorca the same day that my predecessor left on the very same plane," she wiggled her eyebrows suggestively.

"What a strange coincidence," Adam said, a wry smile touching his lips.

"Isn't it just," Daisy agreed, "anyway, here we are, you'll stand here Adam, and Flora you'll walk up the aisle with..?"

"Betty," Flora said happily, "Harry will be Adam's best man and Betty will walk with me."

"Oh, that's so lovely," Daisy seemed slightly overcome for a moment and turned away to dab discreetly at her eyes, "excuse me, I was brought up by my grandmother and it was my dream as a girl that she would walk me up the aisle."

"Oh, I'm sorry," Flora said gently.

"Not at all, not at all," the vicar was quick to compose herself again, "and we can have our organist play for you as you come in Flora, though I'm afraid whatever tune you choose will end up sounding like 'All Things Bright and Beautiful'. Lovely woman, very limited repertoire."

"Oh, I'm sure that'll be grand," Flora smiled, her mood lightening the longer she spent in this place.

"Perfect, so you'll walk up to join Adam…" Daisy continued until they had an overview of the whole service and then they walked past the small, grassy graveyard to the vicarage.

"Oh, I think your car alarm is going off," Adam said, as they reached the door to the vicar's home.

"Oh, my car is parked on Church Street and it doesn't have an alar… ah, that'll be Archie."

"Archie?" Flora and Adam asked in unison.

"Yes, as well as my curate doing a runner, he also left me his rather vocal pet," Daisy replied, her lips pursed in displeasure.

"I certainly have some experience with that!" Flora

laughed, causing Reggie to waddle up and down on her shoulder, chirping happily to himself, evidently realising that he was being spoken about.

"Yes well, this little guy is very good at impersonating sounds. Likes to call himself The Archbishop of York, and thinks he's my own personal alarm clock."

"Oh! He's a mynah bird!" Flora exclaimed as they entered the small vicarage hallway and were met with a dark bird with a very yellow beak perched on a coat stand. The building was much smaller than the vicarage in Baker's Rise and the entrance area too small to accommodate them all, so Daisy led them straight through to the kitchen, her strange pet following her through. His car alarm noises had thankfully stopped but, on seeing the parrot with Flora, he piped up again with a perfect impersonation of an ambulance siren.

"Please excuse him, he's just showing off," Daisy shook her head and shrugged her shoulders in apparent defeat – a gesture Flora knew all too well.

Flora felt Reggie stiffen on her own shoulder and his happy babbling ceased, "Get out of it!" he shrieked, "Get out of it!"

"Now Reggie," Flora spoke softly to try to calm the bird and tapped his beak gently, "it's Ar…Chie. He's a bird, like you. Ar...Chie." She split the syllables to help Reggie learn the name more quickly.

"Ask Me! Ask Me!" Reggie shrieked, trying to repeat her, yet still clearly freaked by the encounter.

"Hmm," Flora said her mind whirring and a sudden feeling of nausea overcoming her.

"Flora, love, do you need to sit down?" Adam asked quickly, perfectly attuned to his fiancée's mood.

"Yes, of course, let's get you sat down," Daisy jumped to action, pulling out a chair as Adam took Flora's elbow and helped her down.

"It's likely the heat, and all the excitement and butterflies," Daisy said kindly, handing Flora a glass of water."

"Perhaps," Flora said, as she took a measured sip, "perhaps."

But she didn't look at all convinced.

NINETEEN

"So, would you like to talk about the funny turn you had back there?" Adam asked as they hurried back towards the inn some half an hour later. They had rushed through tea and cake, with Flora unable to focus on the conversation going on beside her, and Adam sending worried glances her way every few minutes.

"Ah, well, some pieces of the puzzle seem to be fitting together in my head. Or, at least, some ideas that I can't seem to shift."

"And what puzzle would that be?" Adam asked, a rather ominous tone to his voice.

Flora knew that he didn't want her giving any more head space to the deaths at the hotel, and certainly didn't want her getting involved in the investigation again, so she hesitated before she answered, "Some things have been niggling at the back of my consciousness, and, well, I think they've just come to the front."

"I see, well I think we should take some time to talk them through. Not do anything rash, of course, but certainly I want to hear your thoughts."

"Really?"

"Of course. I suppose for selfish reasons, I don't want you preoccupied with anything other than our upcoming wedding, but at the same time you've been perceptive with finding and analysing clues in the past and I trust your evaluations."

"That means… more to me than you realise," Flora stopped walking and kissed her fiancé on the cheek.

"Harry mentioned taking the women into Whitby for the afternoon, so let's head back and we can discuss it over a glass of wine and a pint of ale, just the two of us," Adam said, pulling Flora closer to his side as they walked with his arm around her shoulders.

Reggie still had his feathers in a fluff from his encounter with Archie earlier, and flew ahead, occasionally shrieking "The fool has arrived! Ask Me!" and garnering them more than a few strange looks.

"That'll be perfect," Flora replied, "and I think Reggie could do with a nap in my room!"

"So," Adam began when they were ensconced in a dark corner of the bar area at the inn, "tell me all."

"Well," Flora took a gulp of her red wine and twirled the long stem of the glass between her fingers, "there are two things that I'm thinking, and they both concern the hotel receptionist."

"The second murder victim?"

"Yes, ah maybe I shouldn't cast aspersions when the poor girl is dead now…" Flora twiddled with her hair anxiously.

Seeing the motion, Adam took that hand gently in his own, "Well love, it's just between you and I, so as always you can share anything and it won't go any further."

Emboldened by that knowledge, Flora began, "Well,

Hailey had a strong allergy to animals, whether it was dog fur or bird feathers I'm not sure, but whenever she was in the vicinity of Reggie and Tina she started sneezing uncontrollably – just like that awful florist did this morning. It was that, you see, that triggered me to remember, she was sneezing when I saw her in the doorway to the baking studio just after Ingrid's murder. Yet the animals weren't near her, and hadn't been in the studio. The only place they had been that morning, in fact, was Ingrid's study."

"The room where the woman was murdered?"

"Exactly, which makes me think Hailey must've been in that room after we had stored the pets there for our lesson."

"Well, that's interesting, love, but it's circumstantial at best, nothing that really implicates the receptionist."

"Yes, I know, which is why I guess it was never important enough to come to the front of my mind, except, when paired with my second point…"

"Don't keep me waiting then," Adam took a long draught of his pint and looked at her expectantly.

"This may be just as speculative, I realise that, but Betty said that Ingrid's last words were 'help me' in her own language. I looked that up on my phone at the time and the Swedish would be 'hjälp mig'. It does sound a lot like 'help me', but just as Reggie misheard Archie's name, could Betty not have misheard too?"

"I think I see where you're going with this," Adam said, his expression a lot more solemn now.

"Yes, could Ingrid have said 'Hailey' but what with the gurgled sound from her throat that Betty mentioned it wouldn't have been clear enough..?"

"I think you may be onto something there, love. After all, that chef strongly denied the first murder, didn't he? But what about motive?"

"There I have no ideas. I do wonder if it's linked to whomever Hailey was talking to when I saw her coming out of the kitchen looking all dishevelled that morning."

"Oh, I don't think you've told me about that."

"Well, there isn't much to tell. I had just collected the animals from the laundry room, when Hailey rushed out of the kitchen. Her uniform had looked messy on the day we arrived, with paint splatters and whatnot, but that morning she looked a crumpled mess. Her blouse, that was tightly fitted like everything she wore, and which was normally tucked into her skirt, had been pulled out at the back and was completely creased. She seemed quite frazzled in general that morning, and was away from the front desk for most of the time too."

"Paint you say?" Adam replied, picking up on what Flora felt was the most inconsequential fact of them all, "and tell me, was she wearing this same blouse all day?"

Flora scrunched her brow in concentration for a few seconds before replying, "Actually, later she was wearing a baggy shirt, far too big for her."

"Hmm," Adam rubbed his chin thoughtfully, "now think carefully, love, the times you were in the owner's office and in the laundry room, did you notice anything?"

"What kind of anything?"

"Just something that might be... amiss."

Again, Flora took her time to go back in her memory, "Nothing really, just we seemed to be playing a game of yo-yos with the windows."

"What do you mean by yo-yos?"

"Well, I mean like up-and-down. They were the original sash windows, and whenever we closed the one in the laundry to keep the animals contained, it would be open the next time we went in. The window in Ingrid's office was open when I went to check on the body, too, when it had been closed before to keep the pets safe. Should we go to the police with all this?"

Adam sucked his breath between his teeth, "Okay, as much as I hate to suggest it, love, I think we need to do some investigating of our own back up at the hotel."

A shiver ran up Flora's spine at the thought, whether of nervousness or excitement she couldn't be sure.

If Hailey was a murderer, then she was no threat to them. Nor was Pierre, who remained in police custody. But what if there was still a danger lurking up there? What if their speculations were decidedly off the mark?

Flora didn't voice any of this to Adam, as she didn't want to give him any excuse to say he'd better go alone.

And there was no way she was being left behind.

TWENTY

"I don't generally condone snooping," Adam clarified for about the fourth time as they walked around the side of the hotel building early the next day. The others were making a trip to York, as Betty wanted to visit her namesake, the famous tearoom called Betty's, where she planned to enjoy their signature Fat Rascal. Hence Flora and Adam had reluctantly brought a certain little parrot along with them, making excuses to the others that they were keen to spend some time before their wedding alone.

"And he is hardly going to help us remain incognito," Adam continued.

"I know you don't, and I know he won't," Flora replied tersely, though she stopped short of suggesting they reschedule their secret investigation for later. They hadn't told anyone else of their plans, not wanting to get their friends in trouble if they were caught.

"So, remember, if anyone questions us you think you've left a necklace. The last time you remember having it on was outside with Ingrid, having tea on the patio, okay?"

"Yes Adam, we've been through this," Flora struggled to keep the exasperation from her whispered retort.

"Sorry love, I'm just on edge."

"I know, me too."

"Did you see that 'For Sale' sign out front?" Flora asked quietly.

"I did indeed," Adam's jaw hardened, and he had the steely look she had seen on him previously when investigating a case, "that was fast."

"Wasn't it just!" Flora agreed, as they paused under the window to the late owner's office.

Scanning in all directions and confirming that they were alone, Adam spoke in a hushed voice, "So, this was the window that was open when you found the body? Now, love, walk me along this outside wall until we reach the window to the laundry room."

Flora had never travelled between the two rooms from this side, outside of the building, but it wasn't difficult, as both rooms faced out onto this back area of the hotel, "It's down here, past the baking studio, past the dining room and then the kitchen," Flora whispered as they crouched slightly and hurried along beside the thick shrubbery and bushes which lined the wall.

Reaching the laundry window, Adam stopped and crouched down, leaning forward into the thick greenery until his head had completely disappeared from view.

"Careful, you'll get your face scratched," Flora said, as she set the pet carrier down gently and came to kneel beside her fiancé. The sharp gravel bit into her knees through her sundress, but Flora didn't care once she saw what Adam was now stretching to retrieve.

Adam leant forwards as far as he could, so that his shoulders were engulfed by the plants, whilst Flora also squeezed her head between the branches and watched as her fiancé grabbed a ball of white and pulled it towards them. It required a joint effort to unhook the material as it got snagged on the way out, but after a few moments they had it free.

Flora ignored her painful, creaking knees and looked up at Adam, "Is that..?"

"I believe it is, yes," Adam un-balled the item, which was splattered in dark patches of crusty, dried blood, "the receptionist's blouse."

"Oh my goodness!" Seeing the evidence of Ingrid's demise brought the bile back to Flora's throat and her hands automatically came to her mouth, "that's Hailey's, meaning she must..."

"Yes, it would seem she killed Ingrid, exited through the office window back there, ran along here, and whipped off the evidence before climbing in the laundry window here. I would guess that she just grabbed the first shirt that came to hand, in this case a man's garment hence it swamping her in size. Whole thing looks unplanned though, or at least extremely ill-thought out. Or else the girl's nerves simply got the better of her. Happens more than you'd think, not every murderer is a cold, hard killer."

"Yes, I mean, she dropped the knife, then hid the blouse so close..." Flora felt her hands trembling.

"I do think Betty must've disturbed her."

"Then Tanya, Jean and I must've only just walked

away before she came running down here. A few minutes difference and we would've seen her," Flora felt renewed shock at this new knowledge.

"Well, a few minutes is all it takes in some cases... Blummin heck!" Adam launched himself sideways into Flora, effectively knocking her off balance and then shielded her with his own body, as a huge crash sounded just the other side of him.

For a few seconds afterwards, as dust swirled around them, the couple stayed completely still with Flora extremely glad Reggie's carrier was safely on her other side.

"Adam, what on earth was that?" Flora asked as they slowly straightened up, not that it needed much explanation once she could actually see the source of the noise. A stone statue, identical to others that lined the wall of the old building, and which had previously been attached to the ledge just above the first floor window above them, appeared to have come loose and to have crashed down, narrowly missing the pair. It lay now, smashed to smithereens, with small shards peppering Adam's back.

"My goodness, if you hadn't acted when you did... Adam, your cheek is bleeding!" Flora's whole body was shaking now.

"Just a graze love," he wiped the trickle of blood gingerly with a finger, "you wait here, while I just…" Adam guided a wobbly Flora away from the side of the house, whilst storing the blouse in a plastic bag which he produced from his inside blazer pocket. "In fact, I don't want you waiting out here alone, come with me. Quickly now!"

They rushed to the nearest door on that side, which was the French doors leading from the baking studio. Thankfully, they found these unlocked, and Adam darted inside, followed by Flora who was struggling to hold the pet carrier. Reggie was so distressed that he was now trying to fly inside the case, and the whole thing was jumping erratically in Flora's arms.

"Let him free, love, they clearly know we're here anyway."

"You mean, you don't think the statue fell accidently?" Flora felt her lip wobble as she kept her feet moving on autopilot, unzipped the carrier and released Reggie, who immediately snuggled himself against her chest.

"Absolutely not. It would be too much of a coincidence really, wouldn't it?" Adam said, hurrying up the main staircase with Flora and Reggie following close behind.

The room above their previous location was apparently

empty, though the window stood wide open, and they both peered down onto the concrete carnage below, "Well, someone was here a few minutes ago, and I have a good idea who," Adam said as he hurried across the empty bedroom to the en suite bathroom, presumably to check they were definitely alone in the room.

The bedroom itself looked to have been recently decorated, or at least, half of it was. It reeked of fresh paint and Flora saw two cans of paint and two brushes sitting in the corner.

"Flora! Come here and see this," Adam called, and Flora turned to rush over before remembering Reggie who had settled himself on the open window ledge. Not surprisingly, the little bird refused to go with her.

"I know, I know you're scared. You stay where you can make a quick exit if need be," Flora whispered to her pet, before hurrying to see what her fiancé had found, sending a prayer up that it wasn't another body.

TWENTY-ONE

Thankfully the small bathroom was free of other human life – either alive or dead – and it was just Flora and Adam who stood staring at the wall. One half of the room had been given a fresh coat of paint, but the remainder had been left unfinished, and it was this side that attracted the couple's attention now.

There, in a rather childishly painted heart next to an old mirror, were the initials H and L, joined by a plus sign.

"Oh my goodness! H and L, Hailey and Lars," Flora said immediately, "she was in love with Lars Hansen!" She whipped her mobile phone out of her handbag and began taking photos of the wall to pass to the police.

Adam contemplated the evidence in silence, no doubt going through every single thing they knew about the case in his head, and had just opened his mouth to reply at the same moment a shrieked squawk came from the other room, "Bad bird! Now there's trouble! Secrets and lies!"

"Shut up!" The man's voice, with his distinctive accent, was unmistakable, as Adam manoeuvred himself so that Flora was behind him as he left the bathroom.

"Mr. Hansen," Adam greeted the man who stood opposite him, eyes blazing.

Flora peered over her fiancé's shoulder but made no move to stand alongside him, simply welcoming the flash of green feathers which came to land on her shoulder.

"I will not insult you with the excuse that we are here to look for a missing necklace," Adam began, "as I am sure you saw what we found outside before you launched that statue onto our heads. I'm surprised you didn't think to look for it yourself."

"I have no idea what statue you're referring to, nor what you have found," Lars said, though he looked Adam up and down, as if wondering whether he had Hailey's spoiled blouse hidden about his person.

"That young woman was obviously in love with you," Flora stated, moving forwards alongside her fiancé now, "she was splattered in paint every time I saw her, no doubt from helping you decorate this room. She was distracted on the morning of your mother's murder and had been having a heated moment with someone in the kitchen, whom I now assume to be you. Was she reluctant to follow your murderous orders?"

"Your conjecture is not even interesting," Lars said, "it's boring and simple speculation."

"You can deny it all you want now, but I'm sure the police will be interested in hearing Hailey's motive for the murder – what did you promise her Mr. Hansen? A new life in the country with you? I see you've already put this place up for sale," Adam continued, "meaning that you made arrangements with the estate agents before your mother's death. How strange that you would be able to foresee that happening, don't you think?"

Lars' face had grown red and his teeth were bared, as if the man was silently snarling at them, "I am guilty of nothing!" His voice was raised now, "The police cannot lay any of the blame at my door. What that stupid girl chose to do was up to her, and if that doe-eyed French fool flew off the handle and acted in a fit of jealous rage when he saw her wearing my shirt… well, I'm glad the woman who killed my mother received the same justice."

"Yes, I imagine that extra little surprise worked well in your favour, didn't it? Tied up your loose ends nicely, I'm sure," Adam was clearly trying to rile the man now, Flora thought, "and as for you being blameless, well there is the little matter of our attempted murder outside just now."

"And what if that was me?" Lars spoke with the over-reaching assurance of one who believes they have – quite literally – gotten away with murder, "What if I did bribe Hailey with the promise of marriage and wealth? What if I did siphon off money and put a deposit on a lovely golf retreat, only paying lip service to doing this place up and lifting the odd brush when my mother was looking?" He was bragging now, Flora could tell and it made her feel sick to her stomach, "Who would believe you? Especially now you have Hailey's blouse as evidence that she was the murderer. I bet they'll even find her fingerprints on the knife, stupid girl didn't even have the sense to wear gloves."

"How would you know that?" Adam's voice was as hard as the stone that had nearly killed them.

"What?"

"How would you know that Hailey didn't wear gloves if you weren't with her, at least up until she entered your mother's office?"

"You can prove nothing, now get out of my hotel," Lars said, his lip curled in anger.

"I think we have all the evidence we need," Flora said, assuming an air of confidence she did not feel – inside, her legs felt like jelly and her stomach was like a whirlpool.

"Impossible, I have thought of everything!" Lars declared.

"Maybe, maybe not," Flora replied, jiggling her mobile phone conspicuously, where it still rested in her hand.

"You wouldn't have!" Lars shouted.

"Oh, I believe I have recorded the whole conversation, yes," Flora made to turn for the door, but Lars darted towards her, effectively blocking her exit. As Adam moved to interject himself between the two, Reggie took off from Flora's shoulder, in ominous silence for once, and flew straight for Lars' face, his beak aimed at the man's eyes.

"Argh!" Lars shouted, as the bird hit his face with enough force to send the man staggering backwards.

"Reggie!" Flora screamed, knowing her little bird couldn't come off well from such an impact.

"I've got this, you get outside and call the police," Adam said, "And don't let that phone out of your sight!"

TWENTY-TWO

Flora sat in the waiting room at the emergency vet's surgery with her head in her hands, tears dripping through her fingers. He had really done it this time, her stupid, selfless, heroic little parrot.

Adam had waited at the hotel to give a full statement to the police, whilst the paramedics had turned up to deal with the deep gash just above Lars Hansen's eye. Flora had given a brief explanation of what the video footage contained, had handed over her phone as evidence, and had then been allowed to leave, with her precious bundle wrapped in one of the beautiful cream blankets from the hotel's reception area.

"My Flora," he had chirped on the journey in the taxi,

where Flora had held her special companion to her, willing the journey to go faster. His little voice was so faint, however, that she had to lower her ear to make out the words.

"Mrs. Miller?" The veterinary nurse appeared from a door to the right of the bland waiting room and Flora immediately jumped to her feet, trying to judge from the woman's expression whether the news was good or bad.

"Yes?" The lump in her throat was so large, that only that one word managed to escape her lips.

"I'm afraid Reggie has a broken wing and a concussion, as well as one of his talons having to be removed, and a small crack in his beak which will have to grow out over time."

"But he's alive? I mean, you can fix him?"

"Yes, the vet has been with him, splinting the fracture and of course we'll need to keep him in for observation. He's not out of the woods yet, as with any head trauma, we just have to wait and see, but the vet is confident of a positive outcome."

"He might be... as good as new?" Flora hadn't even dared to hope.

"Time will tell, but it's definitely a possibility, yes."

"Oh thank heavens! Praise be!" Flora exclaimed, tears streaming down her cheeks once again.

"So, it was the chef that killed the young woman in a lust-fuelled haze when he returned to the hotel for his evening shift, but he was not the one that did for the old woman. It was in fact the young woman that killed the old woman, but not really of her own accord. She was pushed into it by the son of the old woman," Harry reiterated the explanation back to them whilst Flora and Adam simply nodded.

"Yes, sadly, her obsession with Lars Hansen was of such magnitude that Hailey thought he was worth killing for," Flora said softly, "what a tragic waste of two lives."

"Isn't it just," Adam agreed, rubbing his thumb gently over the back of Flora's hand.

"And they can't arrest him for anything other than attempted murder?" Tanya asked.

"No, not unless something else comes to light, maybe this wasn't the first time he has killed to get what he wants…" Adam answered slowly, clearly distracted for a moment by his own thoughts, "but at least the police can get to the bottom of it all now. Thanks to my Flora and her fantastic ability to notice the small details. You would've made a great detective, love."

Flora appreciated the compliment, but simply smiled wanly. Her constitution certainly couldn't take doing a job like that day in day out. Besides, Adam's reference to 'my Flora' had her thinking once again about her little parrot who was spending the night across town in the animal hospital. Flora felt… bereft.

"It has been another long day," Jean yawned, her kind eyes looking at Flora, "I think we should all get an early night."

"I'm with you there," Betty said, "My bunions aren't half playing up in this heat…"

"Aaand, it's time for bed," Harry interrupted her, before they were all subjected yet again to the finer details of his wife's podiatry problems.

TWENTY-THREE

Flora looked at her borrowed phone – which Adam had kindly lent her until she received her own back from the police – for the umpteenth time that morning, checking to see if she had missed any messages from the animal hospital. When she had phoned to ask after Reggie first thing, the nurse had told her that he had spent a comfortable night, and had kept everyone who had checked on him entertained with his rather colourful language. Flora could well imagine. At least a return to his usual antics meant the little bird was on the mend, though. Anyway, they had promised to let her know the moment the vet cleared him for discharge, and Flora was on tenterhooks waiting for the call. Even the beautiful view of the tranquil North

Sea, calm waves lapping onto the sand and the joyful sounds of families playing nearby, failed to distract her.

"I'm sure it won't be long now, lass," Betty said from the deckchair next to hers, finishing off the last bite of a cream éclair that Tanya had bought from the local bakers that morning and giving the last tiny bite of pastry to Tina.

"I know, I know," Flora answered, though behind her dark sunglasses she felt her eyes start leaking again, "I'm sure I'll be fine once I've seen him for myself. Anyway, tell me about your visit to York yesterday, I hear you all had a lovely time."

"Oh aye, it was a grand trip out, that's for sure. That Betty's tearoom is something else! Costs a packet, mind you – they didn't even give us a discount when I told them my name's Betty! But the Fat Rascal was glorious, the plumpest, fruitiest scone I've ever had save for my own creations of course, though strictly speaking it's a cross between a rock cake and a scone. Did you know that?"

"No, no I didn't," Flora was struggling to focus on the conversation.

Betty, however, was undeterred, "Then we went into

York Minster and saw the famous stained glass windows – the Rose Window was my favourite, of course, that having been my mother's name."

"Oh, I didn't know that Betty, that's a beautiful name."

"Aye, she was a lovely woman, a real master baker too, she could teach these young'uns a thing or two."

"I'm sure she could," Flora replied, scanning the promenade to see if there was any sign of Harry and Adam returning from their walk. They had seemed very secretive again this morning, and Flora was keen to know why.

"Aye, then we traipsed round the shops looking for wedding outfits for Jean and Tanya. Understandably they both wanted new rigouts for your special day but, well, as you can imagine their tastes are a bit different, which meant two separate lists of shops to visit. My poor bunions, I can tell you…"

Thankfully Tina's barking interrupted their conversation as Flora spied the two men approaching from the other end of the beach.

"Perfect timing, I could do with a cuppa," Jean said, laying her knitting down on her lap and stretching her arms above her head.

"And some cake," Betty added, folding up the wrapper from her éclair and placing it in her handbag until she could find a bin.

"Someone should wake Tanya," Flora said, smiling at her friend, who was snoring lightly in the deckchair next to Jean, her sunhat covering most of her face.

"Poor thing, I think we oldies wore her out yesterday," Jean laughed, tapping Tanya lightly on the arm.

"You two are looking very pleased with yourselves," Betty commented as the two men reached the small group.

She's right, Flora thought, *they couldn't look more like the cat that got the cream if they tried.*

There was no time for questions, however, as at that very moment Flora's phone lit up with the vet's number and she sucked in a quick breath.

"You know he'll be fine, love," Adam reassured as he placed his hand gently on her shoulder.

"I know, it's just…"

"Well, you won't know unless you answer it!" Tanya said, prompting Flora to take the call before it rang off.

"So, here he is," the vet said, bending to open the cage door to retrieve Reggie, "you'll need to keep the wing splinted for at least seven to ten days then have your own vet remove it. Remove any of his usual perches from the home and just put down a soft towel or blanket. There have been no lasting signs of head trauma. Where he tore off the talon requires antibiotic ointment daily, and this is also to be applied on the scales that have come away around the area. As you can see this small area is currently bandaged. I will give you a supply of bandages so that you can remove the old one, apply the ointment, leave it to air dry and then replace the bandage daily. Any questions ask your own vet. Most important, though, is just to keep him calm and quiet."

"Ah, that'll be easier said than done," Flora muttered, feeling somewhat overwhelmed with all of the information. The moment she heard the strong squawk of "My Flora!" however, all of her worries about his aftercare seemed to fade in the face of seeing her little pal again.

"My Reggie!" Flora scooped him from the vet's hands into her own, "My little wounded soldier!"

"I'll just settle up while you pop him in the carrier," Adam said.

"Ah, maybe better just to carry him in a blanket for today so his side doesn't get bashed," the vet said.

"Of course," Flora agreed readily, keen not to be parted from her feathery companion.

After a brief moment where Adam inhaled sharply and his eyes flew out on stalks when seeing the invoice, they gave the vet's team their thanks and hurried from the building.

"I know you and Harry were up to something this morning," Flora said when they were back in the car, Reggie snoozing on her lap.

"Maybe," Adam replied casting a sideways wink in her direction.

"Well?" Flora asked, nerves and impatience warring inside her.

"All will be revealed, my love," is all that Adam would say on the matter, much to Flora's chagrin.

"I'll ask Harry then!" she said petulantly.

"Well, you can try," Adam laughed, his tone full of confidence.

"Hmph," Flora sighed, "I don't like secrets."

"Well, you'll like these," Adam smirked, further infuriating his fiancée, so that it took her a moment or two to realise that he'd spoken in the plural.

"These?" Flora asked, but they were already pulling into Church Street, where Flora was due to meet the other ladies at the vicarage to prepare the wedding meal for the next day.

Adam laughed and kissed her sweetly on the lips, "Go and prepare us a feast," he declared.

"You aren't coming?"

"No, ah, Harry and I thought that it would be wise to stay out of the wa… ah, to go over the plans for tomorrow over a pint at the inn."

"Very wise indeed," Flora muttered as Adam helped her out of the car carefully with her feathery bundle.

TWENTY-FOUR

"Now you just sit there with that cup of Earl Grey and nurse your wee birdie," Jean whispered kindly, passing Flora a vintage floral milk jug across the large farmhouse table in the vicarage's kitchen, "Betty is on one of her missions and… well, it's probably best if we let her get on with it."

As if on cue, the woman herself emerged from the walk-in pantry behind them, marching with purpose, her arms full of different types of flour, of jars of dried fruits and various sugars.

"Are you sure I can't help you, Mrs. Bentley?" The vicar followed in Betty's wake, though the determined woman was already halfway across the kitchen.

"Betty isn't what you'd call a team player," Tanya said bluntly from her spot opposite Flora, "best to let her call on you if you're needed."

"Oh, well," Daisy said, "I mean, my grandmother taught me to bake…"

"Well, then you're a lot more qualified for the task than these two," Betty indicated Flora and Tanya with a jerk of her head. Her small spectacles were perched on her nose, her grey curls tied back in a headscarf, and her apron cords pulled as tightly as could be – she was the picture of a Sergeant Baker, if there is such a thing in the armed forces!

"Well, that's a bit rud…" Tanya began, but fell quiet when Flora gave a sharp shake of her head.

"After all the stress of the last few days, how about we let Betty and Jean do what they enjoy?" Flora said diplomatically, glad for the sit down if she was honest. The last thing she fancied was to be following Betty's orders all afternoon, "Why don't you join us, Daisy?"

"Well, to be honest I'd welcome any distraction from writing Sunday's sermon. I want to go with a theme of 'knowing when it's time to quit' or 'feeling when something isn't God's plan for you,' but it's not going too well."

"Maybe we can help you," Jean said, from the counter where Betty was watching her with hawklike eyes as she cracked eggs into a bowl, "is there a reason you've chosen that particular subject?"

"Well, it's true that if I just listened for what I was meant to say this Sunday, went for a gut feeling, if you will, then that would be easier, and that's certainly been my method in the past. But ah, this topic is more personal. There's a man in the town…"

"Gerald Bunch?" Flora interjected.

"Exactly so, the local florist has, ah, set his sights on me and sees fit to propose at the Sunday morning service once a month like clockwork."

"I take it his feelings are not reciprocated?" Betty asked, not taking her eyes off the currants she was measuring out.

"Far from it," Daisy said, "he is, ah, well…"

"He's a letch," Flora answered for her, detailing her whole short but unpleasant encounter with the man, "keeps referencing making babies with the vicar here."

"You need a court order," Tanya said decisively, "what is it called? Restraining order?"

"Yes, well I wish I could, but as the parish vicar I'm in a rather difficult position," Daisy admitted sombrely, "the Bishop thinks I should persevere with declining him."

"But for how long? That's surely not sustainable," Flora said gently.

"If it were a woman in that high position she would say different," Tanya announced.

"Well, that's as maybe, but for now I'm stuck," Daisy replied, "so I'm trying to use some more subtle tactics to relay the information to him."

"Well, if telling the man outright hasn't worked, then I'm not sure the subtle approach will," Jean said kindly.

A sharp knock on the front door at that moment caused Reggie to startle awake, and a strange little voice in the hallway could be heard saying, "Not today, thank you!"

"Hush Archie," Daisy said, going to answer the door, whilst Reggie shrieked "Missed you!' and "We're a team!" no doubt having been dreaming of his separation from Flora while he was in the hospital.

Flora shushed the parrot as best she could, whilst

keeping one ear on the conversation in the hallway, "That's him," she whispered to the other women.

"Who?"

"Bunch the florist."

"Good afternoon, ladies!" The man in question stalked into the room, his attire identical to the other day and in his arms a box full of Flora's bridal flowers.

"Mr. Bunch, I thought I said my fiancé would collect the flowers," Flora dispensed with the pleasantries. This man set her teeth on edge.

"Indeed, but I wouldn't miss an opportunity to visit our lovely vicar here," he turned to Daisy then – who had followed him into the room and quickly manoeuvred herself to the other side of the table behind Tanya – licking his lips in a most off-putting manner.

"Well, you can put them on the table. We don't need to take up any more of your time," Betty said, her doughy hands firmly placed on her ample hips.

"Oh, I have time to take tea with you delectable females," the man looked to be about to take the seat next to Flora, until the mynah bird from the hallway flew in and landed on his shoulder, "Argh! Allergies!"

The florist shouted, startling Reggie where he was snuggled in his blanket.

"Not that jerk! Stupid git!" Reggie shrieked, while Archie began mimicking the sound of Daisy's morning alarm clock.

"I think it's time you left," Tanya said, rather gleefully, "our familiars have spoken!" She said the second in a spooky voice, implying that one or more of the women had magical powers. Flora thought her friend was enjoying herself maybe a tad too much.

"Daisy, perhaps you could join me outsi…"

"She has baking duties," Betty said solemnly, as if she was speaking about the war effort and not a Victoria sponge and some scones.

"I think your bird might be your secret weapon," Flora said, when the front door was safely locked again after the unwanted visitor.

"You might be right. I've been keeping him at a distance while I decide what to do with the bird, but now, seeing the effect he has…" she said thoughtfully.

"Aye, all you need is to keep him on your shoulder," Betty agreed.

"Well, that might be a bit difficult," Daisy began when the mynah bird, as if to prove her point, started imitating church bells, so loudly that the women covered their ears and Reggie set off on another tirade.

"You have my sympathies," Flora nodded in understanding, trying to calm Reggie once again.

"Anyway," Daisy shook her torso, as if physically brushing off the man's presence, "let's look at these beautiful blooms. That's what my grandmother used to call me, her 'Beautiful Bloom' given that was our surname and all," Daisy blushed and Jean came to put an arm around her.

"She sounds like a lovely lady," Jean said gently.

"She really was," Daisy said sadly, and Flora got the impression there was a big story there, but that was for another day.

TWENTY-FIVE

Flora woke early the next morning, still in a degree of disbelief that this was her wedding day. She had already tried on the outfit that Sally had helped Adam pick for her, and she smiled again as she ran her fingers over the smooth satin. In a shade of subdued purple, which the label called 'Heather', the dress had a V-shaped neckline, a wrap-style waist and a pleated, full skirt which came to just above her ankles. The sleeves came down to her wrists with a slight balloon effect. It matched perfectly with the amethyst necklace which Adam had bought her to wear for Betty and Harry's wedding in the hospital the previous year and with the purple suede Mary-Jane style shoes which he had also purchased. In fact, it was perfect in every way, and Flora felt beautiful.

"First surprise of the day," Adam's voice came through the door as he knocked gently, "there's a lady here to do your hair and make-up."

"Open up, Flora, I've got a bottle of champagne here waiting to be popped while they pamper us!" Tanya chimed in…

And so the special treats began.

All four women had their hair styled and their make-up applied, whilst chatting and giggling like schoolgirls in Flora's room at the inn. Harry had thoughtfully brought Betty's own wedding dress – the one which Flora had chosen while Betty was in the hospital having her hip replaced – and the small, purple embroidered flowers matched Flora's attire perfectly. Jean had chosen a smart dress in navy with a Peter Pan collar and deep cuffs all in lemon. Tanya was very much her own woman in a vintage 1970s dress apparently sourced from a charity shop. Thankfully, it was of the maxi rather than the mini variety, and was covered in a sunflower pattern, which Tanya proudly told them was called 'Sunrise Psychedelia'. It had wide, swishy arms and Tanya had somehow found some orange platform sandals to match.

"You all look so beautiful," Flora gushed, smoothing down her own skirt self-consciously. She still didn't enjoy being the centre of attention.

"Not as gorgeous as you, lovely," Tanya put her arm round Flora's shoulders, having to bend slightly as the platforms had given her an extra few inches in height.

"Your second surprise is here," Adam's voice filtered in from the hotel corridor, "Harry and I are leaving for the church now."

After making sure that Reggie was comfortable in his carrier, which Jean held as if it were made from precious glass, Flora followed her friends down the stairs and outside, where a small crowd had gathered in front of the inn. Keen to see the source of their attention, Flora squeezed through and was shocked by a classic 1930s Rolls Royce Wraith.

"I only told Adam once, months ago, that my dad loved classic cars," Flora's voice faltered, her emotion threatening to ruin her eye make-up.

"Aye, you've got a good'un there," Betty rubbed Flora's back in a maternal fashion, as the chauffeur opened the car door for them solicitously.

"We all tapped in to get you a little wedding present,"

Tanya said, when the friends were in the car and on the short journey to the church.

"Chipped in," Betty corrected her.

"Yes, well," Tanya reached inside her bright yellow, faux fur pouch that she was using as a handbag and produced a small jeweller's gift bag.

"Oh! You shouldn't have," Flora felt the waterworks starting up again as she took out the black box and opened it slowly. Inside were a pair of beautiful amethyst dangling earrings in the shape of teardrops, "Oh my, they are so beautiful!" Flora exclaimed.

"So beautiful," Reggie chimed back from inside the bird carrier, causing them all to laugh.

Emotions ran high, as Betty helped Flora to change into the new set, and they all admired the effect.

"I'm so grateful. Not just for the gift," Flora said, her heart almost bursting, "but for your friendship and support."

"Aw don't you be mekking me cry now," Betty said, dabbing at her eyes with a cotton handkerchief, "not before the service has even started!"

There were waterworks aplenty before the marriage was declared and sealed with a kiss and a well-timed screech of "You sexy beast!" Adam's third and final surprise was matching wedding rings, which he and Harry had found in a jeweller's in Lillymouth. Set in white gold, Flora's had a Celtic design engraved around the outside rim, and two roses entwined on the inside of the band. Adam's was identical, save that his didn't have the secret roses, and it was larger and made from platinum. Flora gasped when she saw them, and was even more surprised when hers fit.

"Meant to be, just like us," Adam had whispered as he slipped it on her fourth finger.

"Thank heavens! Adventure awaits!" A little parrot squawked from Jean's knee, where he had been released from his carrier for the big event.

The church bells rang out – or, rather, it sounded like they did thanks to a clever mynah bird – the organist was as memorably atrocious as Daisy had warned, and the wedding (afternoon) tea was as perfect as Betty had been determined to make it so.

As the others set off for Baker's Rise, with Harry driving Flora's car, the newlyweds headed in the other direction, for a night in Harrogate before returning to Baker's Rise the next evening.

"Just give me twenty-four hours before we go back to our responsibilities," Adam had whispered, when he had shown her the online booking he'd made.

"How did I get so lucky?" Flora asked, resting her head on her new husband's shoulder.

"Oh, I think bigger forces may have been at work," Adam said, looking up towards the Heavens, "and who was I to argue?"

TWENTY-SIX

"You'll put your back out!" Flora giggled, as Adam insisted on carrying her over the threshold of their little coach house the next evening.

"Don't be silly, I'm a man in my prime," Adam joked, whilst going red in the face and making a show of gasping for air.

"I hope Reggie was good for Jean yesterday," Flora mused as she put the kettle on, glad to be back in her own home, "we really should go and get him straight away and then call into the tearoom to make sure everything is okay."

"I'm sure he's being spoilt rotten, let's have a cuppa and a chat first, shall we? And let's leave the tearoom till Monday..." Her husband suggested, putting his arms around Flora's waist and turning her to face him. He kissed her slowly and passionately, until Flora had forgotten all about parrots and everything else in fact.

"Did you mean what you said at sunrise that morning?" Flora asked softly when they were cosied up on the sofa with their hot drinks.

"That I wanted to marry you straight away? I think I proved that, didn't I?" Adam grinned and twiddled with the wedding band on Flora's finger.

"You know that's not what I mean," Flora smiled back, "Just, I understand if you've changed your mind. Such a big decision, you probably shouldn't have made it while you were grieving."

"It was the best time to make it, love," Adam's face suddenly became serious, "life is too short to drag things out or to continue when our hearts have moved on. I definitely want to retire from the police force. I've given them the best years of my life so far, the rest I want to give to you and our life here. Besides, I'm getting too old for all those late nights and chasing bad guys."

"It's not just because it'll be different without Blackett there?"

"Of course it would be, I know that, but no, that's not the main reason for my decision. Old habits will die hard, I realise that, I've already messaged Cluero to suggest they might want to look into the details surrounding the death of Lars Hansen's father – you know, just in case."

"Oh, good thinking! Well, if you're sure, you know I'll support you with whatever you decide."

"I do know, love, thank you, just as I'll be here for you. Was that your books in the box that was waiting by the door?"

"The proof copies, yes, I ordered them before I left. Good job it's not raining, I'll have to have a word with the courier about just dumping them there."

"Aren't you going to open them?"

"Maybe in the morning after church. For now, I just want to stay in this bubble with you and not think about all the tasks that await me. Goodness knows, if you do retire there'll be plenty to keep you busy."

"Good plan," Adam agreed, tucking his new wife closer to his side and kissing the top of her head, "let's not think about the manor house or the tearoom, a rather feisty parrot milking his role of patient, or the new books you've written about him. Fancy an early night?"

"Absolutely," Flora said, already moving to her feet, "let's leave the world outside until tomorrow."

TWENTY-SEVEN

"Flora! I hear huge congratulations are in order! I can't wait to see the photos and hear all about it," Sally gushed after church the next morning.

Flora had already accepted the congratulations of most of her neighbours. Word had obviously spread fast, as they had come armed with cards, flowers and homemade gifts – Flora had a feeling she had Betty to thank for setting the jungle drums a-beating.

"Thank you, and for helping Adam choose the dress, it was beautiful, a real day to remember."

"You're so welcome, anyway must be getting back to finish the Sunday lunch," contrary to her usual enthusiasm, the vicar's wife seemed very keen to make a quick exit now.

"Of course, just, ah about the tearoom?" Flora rested her hand lightly on Sally's arm, "We got back last night and I haven't had a chance to pop in there yet. I trust the ladies managed to find everything okay? And the electronic payment system through my tablet, that worked for them?"

"Well, ah, yes, I think it's fair to say they approached the whole venture with gusto. It was so kind of you to give them the distraction Flora, what with their mother dying so suddenly. The sisters look to be in their late fifties, I think, but they have led a very sheltered life. Between you and me, I think they're going to find it hard to adapt to their new situation."

"Well, they've done me a favour. I brought them back some traditional Yorkshire parkins as a thank you."

"Ah, yes, excellent, just grand…" and Sally drifted away, a concerned look causing her brow to furrow.

"That was a bit odd," Flora turned to Adam, who seemed to be looking off into space – or at least pretending he hadn't heard her, "Adam, did you call into the tearoom when you went to the bookshop to find Harry?"

"Well, I only saw the outside, love, you hadn't long gone away after all, and I don't want you to get mad, okay? They've, ah, worked very hard, lots of gusto."

"Why does everyone keep mentioning gusto?" Flora's eyes narrowed and the hairs on the back of her neck stood on end, "In fact, forget it, let's just head around there now."

"How about dinner in the Bun in the Oven first? Roast beef, Yorkshire puddings, all the veg…"

Flora had already made a beeline for the back of the church, however, her kitten heels stamping a staccato beat on the wooden floor.

The Italian flag outside the door, and the green, white and red bunting in the windows should have alerted Flora before she even stepped foot in the place, but she was so overcome with the feeling of coming home that either her eyes failed to perceive what she didn't want to see, or her brain refused to register the changed details of her sweet tearoom.

Unusually for a Sunday, the lights were on and the door unlocked. Flora, not realising this was the case, began searching in her voluminous holiday handbag for the keys, as the door was flung open to greet them.

"Argh!" Flora shrieked in fright and jumped backwards, banging into Adam.

"Bienvenidos!" Two voices shouted in unison, their Italian accents somewhat lacking.

Flora took a moment to gather her nerves and to take in the sight before her. Normally reclusive, the two sisters were not usually found out and about in the village, hence this was the first time Flora had met them face to face. They each had their short, bobbed hair tied back in Italian flag bandanas, each sported a matching apron and the slightly shorter of the two held out a menu, on the top of which was written 'Trattoria on the Rise.'

"Table for two?" the taller one asked, thankfully no longer adding the accent.

"Actually, I own this place," Flora said, her voice hard and stilted, as her mind wondered if she had somehow entered an alternate universe.

"Oh! You must be Flora, do come in!"

Both shocked and annoyed at being invited into her own space, Flora almost tripped over the doorstep and came face to face with the full vision of their takeover –

nightmarish as it was in that moment. The tables were covered in cloths of one of the three signature colours, matching the bunting that had replaced Flora's gorgeous pastel crochet flags which Rosa had kindly gifted her. And that seemed to be only the beginning. There were cannoli in the display cabinet where before there had been custard tarts, jars of pasta sat where the jams had been, and Reggie's perch had been replaced with… a plastic Leaning Tower of Pisa of all things!

Tears sprang to Flora's eyes as simultaneously her hands balled into fists.

"We were hoping to speak to you about getting a pizza oven…" one of the sisters began, but Flora was already at boiling point.

"Deep breath, love, deep breath," Adam whispered from behind her, "I think they just got a bit carried away. Sally promised me she'd speak to them."

"It was only for one week!" Flora shrieked.

Having the women opposite her looking completely perplexed at her reaction simply added fuel to the fire.

"At least no one's been murdered," Adam said, trying no doubt to lighten the mood.

"Not yet," Flora growled, "not yet!"

Will Flora manage to put her tearoom back to rights without blowing a fuse, or is Little Italy now a permanent fixture in Baker's Rise?

Join Flora and Reggie in, **"The Jam Before the Storm,"** *the eighth instalment in the Baker's Rise Mysteries series.*

Would you like to learn more about Reverend Daisy and her new neighbours as she settles into her new parish in Lillymouth?

"Fresh as a Daisy," *the first instalment in the* **Lillymouth Mysteries** *series will be* **out soon!**

Read on for an excerpt...

AN EXCERPT FROM *FRESH AS A DAISY* – *THE LILLYMOUTH MYSTERIES BOOK ONE*

Daisy Bloom hummed along to the Abba song on Smooth radio, pondering how she might use the lyric 'knowing me, knowing you' this coming Sunday, in the first sermon she would deliver in her new parish. She was barely concentrating on her driving in fact, knowing the roads like the back of her hand as she did. Barely anything changed around here, in this small coastal corner of Yorkshire, and Daisy really wasn't sure if that was a good thing or not. It had been fifteen years since she had left the town of Lillymouth, at the tender age of eighteen, and the newly ordained vicar had not been back since. Indeed, had the Bishop himself not personally decreed this was the parish for her – in some misguided attempt to help her chase away the demons of her past, Daisy presumed – then she suspected that she would not have come back now either.

Positives, think about the positives, Daisy told herself, pushing a finger between her dog collar and her neck to let a bit of air in. The weather was remarkably lovely for early July in the North of England, and Daisy was regretting wearing the item which designated her as a member of the clergy. She had wanted to arrive at her new vicarage with no possibility that they not immediately recognise her as the new incumbent – after that awful time when she turned up as the curate of her last parish, and they had mistaken her as the new church organist. Not helped by the fact that she was tone deaf… She knew she looked very different from the fresh-faced girl who had left town under a black cloud though, so there was a good chance even the older townsfolk wouldn't recognise her.

Anyway, positive thoughts, positive thoughts, Daisy allowed her mind to wander to the shining light, the beacon of hope for her return to this little town – her new goddaughter and namesake, Daisy Mae, daughter of her best friend from high school, Bea. Pulling up outside of the bookshop which her friend owned, and glad to have found a disabled parking spot so close,

A Walk In The Parkin

Daisy was surprised to find she was relieved that the old Victorian building had not changed since she left all those years ago. It still stood tall and proud on the bottom corner of Cobble Wynd and Front Street, it's wooden façade hinting at its age. The building had been a bookshop since Edwardian times, Daisy knew, and she smiled as she saw the window display was filled with baby books and toys – old and new coming together in harmony, something that, according to the Bishop, was far from happening in the town as a whole.

"Daisy!" the familiar voice brought a sudden lump to her throat as Daisy made her way into the relative dimness of the shop, the smell of books and coffee a welcome comfort. The voice of the woman who had been her childhood friend, who had been one of the few to support her when the worst happened all those years ago... *positive thoughts...*

"Bea," Daisy leant her walking stick against the old wooden counter and reached out to hug her friend, careful that her own ample bosom didn't squash the little baby that was held in a carrier at her mother's chest. Wanting to say more, but finding herself unable to speak around her emotion, Daisy tried to put all of the love and affection she could into that physical touch.

"Meet Daisy Mae," Bea said proudly, pulling back and turning sideways so that Daisy could see the baby's face.

"The photos didn't do her justice, Bea, really, she's beautiful." Okay, now the feelings had gone to her eyes, and Daisy tried to wipe them discreetly with the back of her hand. She wasn't this person, who was so easily moved – or at least she hadn't been since she ran and left Lillymouth behind. Daisy had funded herself through training and then worked as a police support officer for victims of violence for almost a decade, before hearing the calling to serve a higher purpose. She had survived assault and injury as part of her previous profession, seen some truly horrible things, and yet had not felt as emotional as she did now. Not since the day she quit this place, in fact…

"Aw, you must be tired from the drive," Bea, tactful and sensitive as always, gave her the perfect 'out', "come and have a cuppa and a sandwich in the tea nook. Andrew just finished refurbishing it for me."

"Thank you, but let me get it for you, are you even meant to be working so soon after the birth?"

"I'm just covering lunchtimes while my maternity cover nips out for a quick bite – well, I think she's actually meeting her boyfriend, she never manages to stick to just the one hour, but, ah, she's young and well read… why don't you hold little Daisy while I get us sorted with something?"

"Oh! I… well, I…"

"You'll be fine, Daisy, you're going to have a lot of babies to hold during christenings, you know! I can't wait for you to christen this little one," Bea chuckled and unfastened the baby pouch, handing the now squirming bundle to the vicar without hesitation once Daisy had lowered herself into a squashy leather armchair.

Wide, deep blue eyes, the colour of the swell in Lillywater Bay on a stormy day looked up at Daisy with surprise and she found herself saying a quick prayer that the baby wouldn't start to scream. Daisy desperately wanted to be a part of this little girl's life, feeling as she did that she might never have a child of her own. What she had seen in her previous profession had put Daisy off relationships for life. As part of the Church of England she was not forbidden from getting married and starting a family – quite the opposite – but Daisy's own feelings on the matter ran deep and dark.

"Here we go," Bea returned with a tray holding a pot

of tea, two china mugs, a plate of sandwiches and some cakes, "you look like you could do with this."

"You aren't wrong there," Daisy felt suddenly and surprisingly bereft as baby Daisy Mae was lifted gently from her arms and placed in a pram in the corner next to them.

"Have you visited the vicarage yet? Nora will be on tenterhooks waiting for you, she'll have Arthur fixing and cleaning everything, poor man!"

"I haven't had that pleasure," Daisy smiled ruefully, "I thought I'd come to visit my two favourites first," Daisy smiled back, knowing she was being slightly cowardly, but Nora Clumping was not a woman to become reacquainted with on an empty stomach. She had been the housekeeper at the vicarage for as long as Daisy could remember, surviving numerous clergy, and she had seemed ancient to Daisy as a girl. She could only imagine how old the woman must be now. She must have a soft side though, Daisy had thought to herself on the journey from Leeds, otherwise she wouldn't have taken Arthur in decades ago and adopted him as her own. Not that that diminished from the woman's formidable presence, however... for someone so slight in stature, she was certainly a powerhouse to contend with!

"Ah, wise choice," Bea agreed, "and if I were you, I'd pick up some fruit scones from Barnes the Baker's before you head up there!"

"Sound advice," Daisy laughed out loud, before remembering the baby who had now fallen back asleep, and lowered her voice to a whisper to joke, "I may be in the church now, but I'm not above the odd bit of bribery where necessary!"

"Just wait till you hear her views on the previous vicar," Bea said, not a small amount of excitement in her voice, "oh how I wish I could be a fly on the wall!"

"Argh," Daisy groaned exaggeratedly into her coffee mug causing her friend to snort.

"I want all the details afterwards," Bea continued, "I'll bet you five pounds that within ten minutes she mentions that time she caught you making a daisy chain with flowers you'd pulled from the vicarage garden."

"I was eight!" Daisy replied in mock protest, even while still knowing her friend was right – nothing was ever forgotten in small towns like these.

"Well, I've still got your back like I did then," Bea said, reaching over to rub Daisy's shoulder conspiratorially, and adding with a wink, "and I'm sure she isn't allowed to give the new vicar chores as punishment!"

Perhaps coming back to this place after so long won't be so bad after all, Daisy thought. *With good friends like this, I can serve the parish, find the justice I seek for Gran and be out of here before the Bishop can say 'Amen.'*

The Bible says 'seek ye first the Kingdom of God' – well, I've done that, now I can seek out a cold hearted killer. They may have gotten away with it for over a decade, but divine retribution is about to be served.

The Jam Before the Storm

Baker's Rise Mysteries Book Eight

Publication Date: November 24th 2022

Put your wellington boots on for this eighth book in the popular Baker's Rise series! Village life has never been cosier – or more deadly!

As the residents of Baker's Rise congregate up at the Houghton's farm for the first ever Autumn Festival, it seems the forecast is not looking good – in more ways than one!

With tears and tantrums, and a few unexpected arrivals to further muddy the waters, storm clouds are clearly gathering on the horizon before the event has even begun!

At least the discovery of a dead body fits the Halloween theme – after all, what's scarier than a corpse?

Packed with twists and turns, colourful characters and a lovely farmyard smell (only joking!), this new mystery will certainly leave you hungry for more!

R. A. Hutchins

Things Cannoli Get Better

Baker's Rise Mysteries Book Nine

Publication Date: May 19th 2023

The scene is set, the cast assembles for a summer soiree to die for – quite literally in this case.

When Flora decides to hire a Murder Mystery troupe to bring a touch of Italian glamour to The Rise, she intends to transport her guests to the Amalfi coast for an evening of spritz and sleuthing.

Never ones to turn down an opportunity for eccentric excitement, the villagers transform themselves… Movie stars, mobsters, even a motor racing legend.

It's all fun and games until someone is actually murdered.

Of course, it wouldn't be Baker's Rise without Reggie wanting a pizza the action, or several puns that are decidedly pasta their sell by date!

Packed with twists and turns, colourful characters and a splash of glitz and glamour, this new mystery will certainly leave you hungry for more!

Fresh as a Daisy

The Lillymouth Mysteries Book One

Coming February 17th 2023

A new mystery series from R. A. Hutchins, author of the popular Baker's Rise Mysteries, combines the charm of a Yorkshire seaside town with the many secrets held by its inhabitants to produce a delightful, cosy page-turner.

When Reverend Daisy Bloom is appointed to the parish of Lillymouth she is far from happy with the decision. Arriving to find a dead body in the church grounds, leaves her even less so.

Reacquainting herself with the painful memories of her childhood home whilst trying to make a fresh start, Daisy leans on old friends and new companions. Playing the part of amateur sleuth was never in her plan, but needs must if she is to ever focus on her own agenda.

Are her new neighbours all as they seem, or are they harbouring secrets which may be their own undoing? Worse still, will they also lead to Daisy's demise?

A tale of homecoming and homicide, of suspense and secrets, this is the first book in the Lillymouth Mysteries Series.

Available for pre-order now!

ABOUT THE AUTHOR

Rachel Hutchins lives in northeast England with her husband, three children and their dog Boudicca. She loves writing both mysteries and romances, and enjoys reading these genres too! Her favourite place is walking along the local coastline, with a coffee and some cake!

You can connect with Rachel and sign up to her monthly **newsletter** via her website at: www.authorrachelhutchins.com

Alternatively, she has social media pages on:

Facebook: www.facebook.com/rahutchinsauthor

Instagram: www.instagram.com/ra_hutchins_author

R. A. Hutchins

OTHER BOOKS BY R. A. HUTCHINS

"The Angel and the Wolf"

What do a beautiful recluse, a well-trained husky, and a middle-aged biker have in common?
Find out in this poignant story of love and hope!

When Isaac meets the Angel and her Wolf, he's unsure whether he's in Hell or Heaven.
Worse still, he can't remember taking that final step. They say that calm follows the storm, but will that be the case for Isaac?

Fate has led him to her door,
Will she have the courage to let him in?

"To Catch A Feather" (Found in Fife Book One)

When tragedy strikes an already vulnerable Kate Winters, she retreats into herself, broken and beaten. Existing rather than living, she makes a journey North to try to find herself, or maybe just looking for some sort of closure.

Cameron McAllister has known his own share of grief and love lost. His son, Josh, is now his only priority. In his forties and running a small coffee shop in a tiny Scottish fishing village, Cal knows he is unlikely to find love again.

When the two meet and sparks fly, can they overcome their past losses and move on towards a shared future, or are the memories which haunt them still too real?

These books, as well as others by Rachel, can be found on Amazon worldwide in e-book and paperback formats, as well as free to read on Kindle Unlimited.

HISTORICAL FICTION UNDER THE PEN NAME *ANNE HUTCHINS*

"Finding Love on Cobble Wynd"

A small coastal town in North Yorkshire is the setting for these three romantic stories, all set in 1910.
As love blossoms for the residents of Lillymouth, figures from their past, mystery and danger all play a part in their story.
Will the course of true love run smooth, or is it not all plain sailing for these three ordinary couples?

Lose yourself in these sweet tales of loves lost and found:

The Little Library on Cobble Wynd

Considered firmly on the shelf, Bea comes to the Lilly Valley looking for a fresh start. She finds more companionship than she ever hoped for in Aaron and his young daughter, but is heartbreak hiding on the horizon?

A Bouquet of Blessings on Cobble Wynd

When florist Eve discovers that her blossoming attraction for the local vicar may be mutual, she is shocked when his attentions run cold. Could danger be lurking in the shadows?

Love is the Best Medicine on Cobble Wynd

An unexpected visitor turns Doctor William Allen's world upside down and sets his pulse racing in this tale of unwanted betrothal.

HISTORICAL FICTION UNDER THE PEN NAME *ANNE HUTCHINS*

"A Lesson in Love on Cobble Wynd"

In 1911, fiercely independent school teacher Florence Cartwright finds herself taking up lodgings in the home of widower and local constable, Robert Hartigan.

Whilst her host remains in an oblivious stupor, Florence does her best to help his three children with their own problems, putting herself in danger in the process.

When higher powers force the couple to form a relationship much closer than either of them would wish, will they be able to overcome their own frustrations and resentments, and move on to something more fulfilling for them both?

Whilst this second book in the Cobble Wynd series does feature some familiar characters from the first book, this story can certainly be read as a standalone novel.

HISTORICAL FICTION UNDER THE PEN NAME *ANNE HUTCHINS*

"Escaping Love on Cobble Wynd"

This story is a prequel to Finding Love on Cobble Wynd by Anne Hutchins.

It is the tale of how Barnabus Willoughby-Smythe, great-uncle to Beatrix and known affectionately as Uncle Banby, came to own the bookshop at the bottom of Cobble Wynd in the town of Lillymouth.

Set in 1836, in the Regency era, it is a tale of love and loss, of adventure and misfortune.

R. A. Hutchins

Printed in Great Britain
by Amazon

47451389R00129